A galaxy of rea

Episode I: The Phantom Menace
Episode II: Attack of the Clones
Episode III: Revenge of the Sith
Episode IV: A New Hope
Episode V: The Empire Strikes Back
Episode VI: Return of the Jedi

THE LAST OF THE JEDI

The Desperate Mission
Dark Warning
Underworld
Death on Naboo
A Tangled Web
Return of the Dark Side
Secret Weapon
Against the Empire
Master of Deception
Reckoning

THE EMPIRE STRIKES BACK

STAR WARS

EPISODE V

THE EMPIRE STRIKES BACK

Ryder Windham
Based on the story by George Lucas and the screenplay
by Lawrence Kasdan and Leigh Brackett

SCHOLASTIC INC.
New York   Toronto   London   Auckland   Sydney
Mexico City   New Delhi   Hong Kong   Buenos Aires

ISBN-13: 978-0-439-68124-7
ISBN-10: 0-439-68124-3

22 21 20 19 18 17   13/0

Printed in the U.S.A.
First printing, October 2004

A long time ago, in a galaxy far, far away. . . .

During the Battle of Yavin, Sith Lord Darth Vader piloted his own Imperial TIE fighter to defend the Death Star space station against a Rebel Alliance assault. While engaged in a dogfight with an X-wing starfighter, he sensed the enemy pilot was strong with the Force. Vader was about to fire upon the X-wing when he and his two wingmen were attacked by a Corellian YT-1300 transport. Vader survived, but his damaged TIE fighter went spinning out of control. Seconds later, the Death Star was blown into a billion pieces.

After Darth Vader brought his crippled spacecraft to an Imperial outpost, he began his investigation. He did not have to identify the Corellian transport. He'd seen it before, when it had been captured by a Death Star tractor beam and deposited in hangar 3207. The transport had been readily identified as the *Millennium Falcon*: the same ship that had eluded Imperial soldiers on Tatooine during their search for an R2 unit that had carried the plans for the Death Star.

Among the *Millennium Falcon*'s passengers from Tatooine was Vader's former Jedi Master, Obi-Wan Kenobi. On the Death Star, Kenobi's allies succeeded in their mission to rescue Princess Leia Organa, the Rebel leader who'd placed the Death Star plans in the R2 unit. Because Darth Vader had once lived on Tatooine, he was nagged by two questions: How long had Obi-Wan been there? And why?

CHAPTER 1

The lone Star Destroyer traveled silently across interstellar space with the precision of a massive dart. An *Imperial*-class warship, it measured 1,600 meters long from its aft ion engines to its sharp-tipped bow, and was equipped with enough firepower to reduce a civilization to ashes. Even without its sixty turbolaser batteries and equal number of ion cannons, the wedge-shaped starship looked like it was ready to cut through anything in its path. The ship's name was the *Avenger*; its commanding officer was Captain Needa.

The *Avenger* arrived at its designated coordinates, then deployed its cargo of hyperdrive pods from a recessed launch bay. Each 3.4-meter-long pod was programmed to travel thousands of light-years on a one-way trip to a specific destination, never to return to the *Avenger* or any other Imperial ship.

Across the galaxy, other Star Destroyers carried

out the same task, releasing hyperdrive pods into space. Soon, thousands of pods were racing off to almost as many worlds, including planets and moons that had yet to be conquered by the Empire. Each pod contained a probot, a probe droid engineered for long-range covert surveillance. Each probot had a single purpose: to find the Rebel Alliance's new base.

The *Avenger*'s pods were targeted for three planetary systems: Allyuen, Tokmia, and Hoth. The Empire had little information regarding Allyuen and Tokmia, and only slightly more for Hoth, a blue-white sun that was orbited by six planets and a wide asteroid belt. According to an old navigational chart, Hoth's inner five planets were lifeless; the outermost planet — also named Hoth — was covered entirely by snow and ice, and was orbited by three nameless moons. Because of the sixth planet's thin atmosphere and close proximity to the asteroid field, it was also frequently battered by meteors.

Speeding through space, a pod arrived in orbit of the ice world. It automatically applied emergency braking thrusters, allowing Hoth's gravity to pull it down through the thin atmosphere. The pod streaked downward until its journey ended on the planet's surface, where it smashed through layers of snow and impacted along the upper slope of a high ravine.

As smoke billowed from the impact site and darkened the surrounding snow, the pod opened to reveal the probot's armored form. Equipped with a repulsorlift and silenced thrusters, the probot had a wide, sensor-laden head that rested upon a cylindrical support body, under which dangled four manipulator arms and a high-torque grasping arm. Although the probot's primary function was to gather and transmit data for the Empire, it was also equipped with a single defense blaster.

Activating its repulsorlift, the black probot rose up through the smoke and went immediately to work. It used its sensors to scan for Alliance transmissions and to survey the terrain, seeking signs of life and habitation. The probot hovered momentarily as it gathered and analyzed data, then moved on, gliding noiselessly through the chilled air . . . unknowingly coming closer and closer to the Rebel base.

Luke Skywalker, wearing an Alliance-issued insulated patrol suit, rode his two-legged snow lizard, a tauntaun, over a windswept ice slope on Hoth. A thin layer of snow had built up on Luke's protective green-lensed goggles, so he momentarily released one gloved hand from the reins to swipe at the goggles and clear his vision.

Luke was looking for wild tauntauns, wampa ice monsters, and any other of Hoth's few indigenous creatures. Sensors were being planted for the Alliance's regional warning network, which would anticipate

Imperial or alien intruders, and it was Luke's job to make sure that no native beasts might accidentally damage them. But from what Luke could see, there wasn't any sign of life amidst the frozen wastes, not even tracks. In every direction, all he saw was white.

Luke felt about as far as he could get from his homeworld, the desert planet Tatooine — not merely because of the great distance between the two planets or their dramatically different climates. So much had changed since he'd joined the Rebellion. He was no longer the boy who'd felt stuck on a moisture farm, who only dreamed of adventures on far-off worlds. He had become a warrior, a hero of the Rebel Alliance, and his adventures had exceeded his dreams.

Yet the price had been unfortunately high. Uncle Owen and Aunt Beru were dead. So was his childhood friend Biggs Darklighter, along with many other brave Rebel pilots who'd fought in the Battle of Yavin. Luke remembered them all, but tried not to think about them too much. It was more in his nature to think of the future than dwell on the past.

But he couldn't stop thinking about Ben, the Jedi Knight, who had served so briefly as Luke's mentor in the ways of the Force.

I still miss him, Luke thought. *I wish I'd gotten to know him better on Tatooine, even though Uncle Owen would have tried to stop me. I could have learned so much. . . .*

Luke knew he needed to focus on his assignment, so he pushed aside his thoughts and guided the tauntaun along a snow-covered ridge. He reined the gray-furred beast to a stop, and it exhaled through its lower pair of nostrils, steaming the air and fogging Luke's goggles. Luke lifted the goggles over his cap's visor, then squinted at the surrounding whiteness.

His keen eyes sighted a streak of light that plummeted from the sky and slammed into the top of a nearby slope, close enough that he could hear the impact. Luke removed his electrobinoculars from his utility belt and peered through the lenses to see a magnified image of smoke rising from the impact site. Just another meteorite on Hoth? Luke wasn't sure.

He lowered the electrobinoculars and returned them to his belt, then brushed snow from the back of his left glove to reveal a comlink transmitter. As he activated the transmitter, his tauntaun shifted nervously beneath him.

"Echo Three to Echo Seven," Luke said into the comlink. "Han, old buddy, do you read me?"

Luke listened to some brief static, then heard the familiar voice of his friend, Han Solo. "Loud and clear, kid. What's up?"

Luke looked around, trying to catch sight of Han, who was also riding a tauntaun. Han's assignment had been to plant the warning sensors.

Luke said, "Well, I finished my circle. I don't pick up any life readings."

"There isn't enough life on this ice cube to fill a space cruiser," Han commented over the comlink. Luke grinned, then caught a brief glimpse of Han's mounted figure before he vanished into the snowy distance. As he departed, Han added, "The sensors are placed. I'm going back."

"Right," Luke said. "I'll see you shortly. There's a meteorite that hit the ground near here. I want to check it out. It won't take long."

Luke switched off his comlink, and his tauntaun snorted nervously. "Hey, steady, girl," he said, reining back. "Hey, what's the matter? You smell something?"

Suddenly, there was a monstrous howl. Luke turned quickly to face a massive wampa, its jaws flung open to display fiercely sharp teeth. A huge, clawed paw slammed into Luke, knocking him from his saddle. He was unconscious before he hit the snow.

Echo Base, the comm-unit designation for the Alliance's command headquarters on Hoth, was a vast network of passages and caves concealed within a glacial mountain. Some of the underground chambers had formed naturally over thousands of years, but most had been carved from the ice in a matter of weeks, thanks to the Alliance Corps of Engineers and their industrial lasers. The base had quickly become home to several thousand Rebel soldiers, technicians, and pilots. It also served as the temporary accommodations for two lapsed mercenaries: Han Solo, captain of the *Millennium Falcon*, and his first mate, Chewbacca the Wookiee.

Although Han and Chewbacca had worked steadily with the Alliance in the three years since the Battle of Yavin, neither had formally enlisted. This was one reason why Han, unlike Luke, wore a dark, fur-lined heavy-weather parka instead of an Alliance uniform. The other reason was that Han thought he looked better in his own clothes.

Returning from his assignment, Han rode his tauntaun up to the mouth of an enormous ice cave, the north entrance of Echo Base. He kept the tauntaun moving at a fast trot as they entered.

The cave had been transformed into a low-ceilinged hangar for starships. Dozens of Rebel soldiers were at work, some busily securing the base while others worked on vehicles. Han steered his tauntaun past a group of Rebel troopers who were unloading supplies, and brought the tauntaun to a stop next to a pair of waiting handlers. They grabbed the beast's reins, and Han dismounted in one smooth motion. Landing on the snow-covered floor, he felt a stinging sensation in his legs, which — despite his insulated boots and leggings — were cold and stiff from riding. As he stepped away from his tauntaun, he pushed his parka's hood back, removed his snow goggles, and kept moving to get the blood circulating in his legs.

Han walked deeper into the hangar. He passed teams of technicians who were adding repulsor-coil heaters to T-47 airspeeders to prevent the motors from freezing, effectively transforming the vehicles into what the Rebels had nicknamed "snowspeeders." A battle-damaged X-wing was also under repair. Han had to be careful not to bump into any Rebels or trip over an astromech droid as he stepped over the power cables that snaked across the floor.

Han finally reached his own ship, the heavily modified Corellian transport. From the hangar floor, he looked up to see Chewbacca sitting atop the *Falcon*'s starboard mandible. Chewbacca, a tall, brown-furred Wookiee, was using one hand to shield his eyes with a pair of welding goggles — the goggles' strap was too small to fit around the Wookiee's broad head — while the other hand operated a fusioncutter. Sparks flew where the fusioncutter's plasma beam met the *Falcon*'s hull.

"Chewie!" Han called out, but the Wookiee didn't stop working. "Chewie!" he called again — to no avail. Either the surrounding noise was too much or the Wookiee was ignoring him. "Chewie!" he yelled a third time.

The Wookiee lowered the goggles and unleashed a series of harsh, irritated growls.

"All right, don't lose your temper," Han said. "I'll come right back and give you a hand."

Han changed out of his cold-weather gear, which reeked of the tauntaun's oily fur, and put on fresh clothes, including a black, long-sleeved jacket that went well with his frame. After changing, he walked through a narrow-walled passage and stepped down into the Echo Base command center.

Laser-cut skylights in the low, icy ceiling provided natural illumination for the room. Han looked around and saw Rebel controllers and droids setting up electronic equipment and monitoring radar signals. Most of the comm-scan computer stations, flat-screen monitors, and even the chairs had been used on Yavin 4, but because of Hoth's climate, the command center was more tightly packed to conserve heat. All the Rebels wore white insulated uniforms, gloves, and gray snowboots.

Han caught sight of Princess Leia Organa, who wore a heated vest over her white jumpsuit. She looked away from her console and spotted him immediately. He held her gaze for a second before he broke eye contact.

The commander of the Alliance ground and fleet forces in the Hoth star system, General Rieekan, glanced up from a console and said, "Solo?"

"No sign of life out there, General," Han reported. "The sensors are in place. You'll know if anything comes around."

Rieekan, looking tired and older than his years, read the data displayed on the console as he asked, "Commander Skywalker reported in yet?"

"No," Han said. "He's checking out a meteorite that hit near him."

"With all the meteorite activity in this system, it's going to be difficult to spot approaching ships," Rieekan said, his eyes still on the console.

"General, I've got to leave," Han said. "I can't stay here anymore."

"I'm sorry to hear that."

"Well, there's a price on my head. If I don't pay off Jabba the Hutt, I'm a dead man." Han didn't have to explain further. Everyone at Echo Station knew that Han had been a smuggler, and that one former client — a notorious Hutt crimelord on Tatooine — had placed a bounty on his head after he'd failed to reimburse the Hutt for a spice shipment he'd dumped to avoid Imperial arrest. The Alliance had given Han more than enough credits to repay Jabba, but the Rebels had also kept him very busy since the Battle of Yavin. Unfortunately, Hutts were not known for their patience.

"A death mark's not an easy thing to live with," Rieekan commented. Looking away from the console, he faced Han. "You're a good fighter, Solo. I hate to lose you." The two men shook hands.

"Thank you, General," Han said. As he turned away from Rieekan, he caught the gaze of Princess Leia again. There was tension in her face, somehow made more severe by the way her hair was braided and tied across her head. Looking at her expression, Han had no trouble imagining she was concerned about him.

Han approached Leia and said, "Well, Your Highness. I guess this is it."

"That's right," Leia replied, her voice cooler than the air.

Taken aback, Han said, "Well, don't get all mushy on me. So long, Princess." He turned away and walked straight for an adjoining laser-cut corridor.

"Han!" Leia shouted, following him into the hall.

Han stopped and turned to face her. "Yes, Your Highnessness?"

"I thought you had decided to stay," Leia said, her voice betraying her disappointment in his decision.

"Well, the bounty hunter we ran into on Ord Mantell changed my mind."

"Han, we need you!"

Han gave her a quizzical look, and echoed, "We need?"

"Yes."

"Oh, what about *you* need?"

"I need?" Leia said, apparently baffled. "I don't know what you're talking about."

Fed up, Han shook his head. "You probably don't." He turned away and headed off through the corridor.

Walking fast to follow Han, Leia said, "And what precisely am I supposed to know?"

Without breaking his stride, Han kept his eyes forward and said, "Come on! You want me to stay because of the way you feel about me."

"Yes," Leia said from behind. "You're a great help to us. You're a natural leader —"

Han stopped and whirled on Leia. "No!" he said, jabbing a finger at her for emphasis. "That's not it. Come on." Leia gaped. Han grinned, then raised a thumb to gesture at his face and said, "Aahhh — uh-huh! Come on."

Leia stared at him for a moment, then said, "You're imagining things."

"Am I?" Han said. "Then why are you following me? Afraid I was going to leave without giving you a good-bye kiss?"

Outraged, Leia spat out, "I'd just as soon kiss a Wookiee."

"I can arrange that," Han replied. As he turned and stormed off down the corridor, he added, "You could use a good kiss!"

Struck speechless, Leia stood there and watched him go. What could she say to him that she hadn't said before? *We're at war with the Empire*, she thought. *There's so much at stake for the Rebellion. I don't have time for . . . for Han Solo's nonsense!*

Later at Echo Station, the golden droid C-3PO and his astromech counterpart, R2-D2, walked through a corridor that led to the main hangar. As they rounded a corner, R2-D2 emitted a flurry of accusatory beeps.

"Don't try to blame me," C-3PO replied testily. "I didn't ask you to turn on the thermal heater. I merely commented that it was freezing in the princess's chamber."

R2-D2 rotated his domed head and responded with a defensive beep, prompting C-3PO to exclaim, "But it's *supposed* to be freezing. How are we going to dry out all her clothes? I really don't know."

R2-D2 beeped in protest, which only made C-3PO more agitated. "Oh, switch off," he said as they entered the hangar.

They approached the *Millennium Falcon*, where they found Han and Chewbacca working on the freighter's central lifters. Han was back in his cold-weather gear, which was now soiled with grime and oil as well as smelling of tauntaun.

"Why did you take this apart now?" Han yelled at Chewbacca. "I'm trying to get us out of here, and you pull both of these —" Words failing him, he gestured at the lifters.

"Excuse me, sir," C-3PO interrupted.

Han said to Chewbacca, "Put them back together right now."

C-3PO tried again. "Might I have a word with you, please?"

"What do you want?" Han snapped, not bothering to hide his irritation.

"Well, it's Princess Leia, sir. She's been trying to get you on the communicator."

"I turned it off," Han said, staring down the droid. "I don't want to talk to her." The way Han said it, he made it clear that he wanted this conversation to end immediately.

"Oh," said C-3PO. "Well, Princess Leia is wondering about Master Luke. He hasn't come back yet. She doesn't know where he is."

"I don't know where he is either," Han fumed, angered that the droid wasn't gone already.

"Nobody knows where he is," C-3PO stated.

That got Han's attention. "What do you mean, 'nobody knows'?"

C-3PO stammered, "Well, uh, you see . . ."

"Deck officer!" Han called out, looking away from C-3PO to find the Rebel officer in charge of docking bay operations. "Deck officer!"

"Excuse me, sir," C-3PO interjected. "Might I inqu —"

Han abruptly put his hand over C-3PO's mouth as

the deck officer ran to them. The deck officer looked at Han and said, "Yes, sir?"-

"Do you know where Commander Skywalker is?"

"I haven't seen him. It's possible he came in through the south entrance."

"'It's possible'?" Han repeated skeptically, and the deck officer realized how feeble his statement had sounded. Han continued, "Why don't you go find out? It's getting dark out there."

"Yes, sir," answered the deck officer, who ran off to find his assistant.

Han removed his hand from C-3PO's mouth. The droid said, "Excuse me, sir. Might I inquire what's going on?"

Concerned and not really listening, Han replied, "Why not?"

Han sauntered off, leaving Chewbacca and the droids behind. C-3PO shook his head and said, "Impossible man. Come along, Artoo, let's find Princess Leia. Between ourselves, I think Master Luke is in considerable danger."

Han made his way to the chamber where the tauntauns were stabled, near the base's north entrance. Several exhausted Rebel scouts rested in the ice-walled chamber . . . but Luke wasn't among them. Han was trying to think of where else Luke might be when the deck officer and his assistant hurried toward him.

"Sir," said the deck officer. "Commander Skywalker hasn't come in the south entrance. He might have forgotten to check in."

"Not likely," Han said. "Are the speeders ready?"

"Er, not yet," said the deck officer. "We're having some trouble adapting them to the cold."

"Then we'll have to go out on tauntauns," Han said. Before anyone could protest, Han turned and headed for the snow lizards.

The deck officer was aghast. Tauntauns were indigenous, but they were hardly invulnerable to the cold, and what Han Solo was about to do was pure madness. Hoping to maintain some control of the situation, the deck officer called after Solo, "Sir, the temperature's dropping too rapidly."

"That's right," Han said without looking back. "And my friend's out in it."

As Han approached the tauntaun he'd ridden earlier, the assistant officer said, "I'll cover sector twelve. Have comm control set to screen alpha."

The deck officer watched Han climb onto the snow creature's back and said, "Your tauntaun'll freeze before you reach the first marker."

"Then I'll see you in hell!" Han replied. He dug his heels into the tauntaun's side, and raced out of the cave into the bitter night.

CHAPTER 2

Luke Skywalker didn't know if he'd emerged from unconsciousness on his own or in response to the wampa's echoing howl. As he opened his eyes and took in his surroundings, he knew he was in serious trouble.

He was hanging upside down. In a cave. His entire body hurt. And he was very, very cold.

He struggled to get his bearings. A chill against the back of his neck suggested the cave's entrance was behind him. Icy stalactites and stalagmites, resembling many rows of teeth, obscured his view of the cave's dim interior. He couldn't see the wampa, but he could hear the snap of bones breaking, and chewing sounds. Judging from what he heard, Luke knew the wampa wasn't very far away.

Straining his aching muscles, Luke twisted his torso and neck to look up at the cave's ceiling. His booted feet were embedded in the ice. He strained his arms up and tried to work his legs out, but the ice was too thick, and he didn't have any leverage. He let his body slump and stretched his arms down, but he was suspended just high enough that he couldn't touch the floor. To free himself, he'd have to blast his way out, or . . .

He remembered his lightsaber. He reached to his belt, but the lightsaber was gone. *Oh, no! Don't tell me it's lost!* Luke angled his head, and spotted the lightsaber half buried in the snow on the floor below him.

He stretched out his arm, but the lightsaber was beyond his reach. Fortunately, Luke had another resource: the Force.

According to Ben, the Force was an energy field created by all living things. It surrounded and penetrated everything, binding the galaxy together. Since the Battle of Yavin, Luke had also learned that the Force could be utilized for moving small objects.

Still suspended from the cave's ceiling, Luke extended his right hand toward the lightsaber. He tried to envision the weapon rising from the snow and arriving into his waiting glove. But nothing happened.

Luke was far from mastering the Force, or even fully understanding it, but he had a feeling that he might be trying too hard. He closed his eyes and relaxed his muscles. He also did his best to remain calm, for in the recesses of his awareness, he sensed that the wampa was moving in the cave. *Did the wampa hear me trying to wrench myself free of the ice?* Luke no longer heard the sound of the creature's chewing.

Luke stopped thinking about the wampa. Again, he extended his hand and gazed upon the lightsaber in the snow. *The Force binds us. . . .*

He heard the approaching wampa's heavy footsteps.

The Force calls my lightsaber to me. . . .

The lightsaber shot out of the snow and into Luke's hand. Luke activated the weapon, and its blue energy beam blazed to life. As he raised the blade to cut through the ice that bound his legs, the wampa lunged for him.

The lightsaber sliced through the ice, and Luke kept the weapon activated as he tumbled to the cave's floor. He sprang to his feet just as the wampa was about to pounce, and swung the lightsaber hard. In a single motion, he cut off the monster's right arm. The severed limb landed on the snow with a muffled thud. Howling in pain, the wampa clutched at its open wound.

Not wasting a precious second, Luke deactivated the lightsaber and scurried away from the wailing beast. He moved by instinct, pushing his way through snow and ice until he tumbled out through the mouth of the cave and into . . .

A blizzard.

When I wanted to leave Tatooine, I never bargained for this.

Dazed and lost, Luke pressed on, leaving the cave far behind as he moved deeper into the storm.

The snowfall was increasingly heavy at Echo Base, where R2-D2 stood just outside the base's north entrance. Ignoring the cold flakes that were collecting on his cylindrical body, the astromech adjusted the slender scanner antenna that protruded up from a panel on his domed head. The antenna was topped by a life-scan sensor, and even though he hadn't picked up any signals so far, R2-D2 wasn't ready to give up. Still, he couldn't help but emit some worried beeps.

"You must come along now, Artoo," said C-3PO, who'd been standing watch with his friend. "There's really nothing more we can do. And my joints are freezing up."

R2-D2 beeped, long and low.

"Don't say things like that!" C-3PO cried. "Of course we'll see Master Luke again. And he'll be quite all right, you'll see." As C-3PO turned and headed back through the hangar entrance, he muttered, "Stupid little short-circuit. He'll be quite all right."

R2-D2 let out a mournful beep, but remained outside, sensors on full alert.

*   *   *

Except for his own gloved hands and the back of his tauntaun's head, Han Solo could barely see anything but falling snow. He knew that finding Luke in this environment was next to impossible, but if he didn't try, Luke was as good as dead.

So Han continued looking and kept the tauntaun moving. Eventually, they arrived near a glacial rise that shielded them slightly from the wind. There, Han let the animal rest while he dismounted, carrying a portable scanner from his utility pack.

Han extended the scanner's antennae and tried to pick up any readings. There were no life-forms within the scanner's limited range and no incoming comm transmissions, but there was plenty of interference from the storm. Han carried the scanner back to the tauntaun and climbed onto his saddle.

In the hangar at Echo Base, a Rebel lieutenant walked up to his commanding officer, Major Derlin, and said, "Sir, all the patrols are in. Still no —"

Major Derlin raised a hand to caution the lieutenant, who then noticed that Princess Leia stood nearby, watching them and listening. The lieutenant gulped, chose his words carefully, and said, "Still no contact from Skywalker or Solo."

Chewbacca, R2-D2, and C-3PO were near the cave's entrance. Hearing the lieutenant's report, C-3PO turned and approached the princess. "Mistress Leia,

Artoo says he's been quite unable to pick up any signals, although he does admit that his own range is far too weak to abandon all hope."

Major Derlin said, "Your Highness, there's nothing more we can do tonight. The shield doors must be closed."

Leia wished she could blink her eyes and wake up from this nightmare, but she knew she wasn't dreaming. Luke and Han really were out there somewhere in sub-freezing temperatures, and unless she wanted the cold to spread throughout Echo Base, the shield doors couldn't remain open. She found herself speechless, and cast her gaze at the floor as she nodded to Major Derlin. It had to be done.

"Close the doors," Derlin ordered.

"Yes, sir," said the lieutenant.

At the mouth of the cave, two thick metal doors rumbled along their tracks as they converged to close off the entrance. Chewbacca moaned, and R2-D2 spat out a complex series of beeps.

Addressing Leia, C-3PO said, "Artoo says the chances of survival are seven hundred and twenty-five . . . to one."

With a loud boom, the doors locked in place and sealed off the cavern. Chewbacca threw his head back and let out a suffering howl.

C-3PO reconsidered his last statement, and

added, "Actually, Artoo has been known to make mistakes . . . from time to time."

Leia walked off, and C-3PO returned to R2-D2. "Oh, dear, oh, dear," said the golden droid. He patted R2-D2's dome, trying to comfort the distressed astromech. "Don't worry about Master Luke, I'm sure he'll be all right. He's quite clever, you know . . . for a human being."

Luke lay facedown in the snow, nearly unconscious. He didn't want to give up, but the cold had given him little choice. Unable to move or feel, and barely able to think, he was waiting for the inevitable when he heard a voice.

"Luke . . . Luke."

Luke recognized the voice. He hadn't heard it since the Battle of Yavin, when it had urged him to trust his feelings and use the Force to destroy the Death Star. Slowly, Luke raised his head. A short distance away from him stood the shimmering, spectral form of Obi-Wan Kenobi. To make sure he wasn't hallucinating, Luke said aloud, "Ben?"

"You will go to the Dagobah system," Ben said.

"Dagobah system?" Luke repeated. *I'm not hallucinating. I'm sure of it.*

"There you will learn from Yoda, the Jedi Master who instructed me."

Luke groaned as he tried not to go into shock. "Ben . . . Ben."

Ben disappeared — but a lone tauntaun rider materialized where he had been and approached Luke's position. Luke's eyes closed and he passed out in the snow.

Fortunately for Luke, the tauntaun rider was not a hallucination, either. Han Solo slid off his mount and trudged as fast as he could to Luke's motionless body. Behind him, his tauntaun let out a low, pitiful bellow.

"Luke!" Han said, taking hold of his friend. "Luke! Don't do this, Luke. Come on, give me a sign here." He leaned close to Luke's face to make sure he was still breathing. He was, but just barely.

Han was trying to think about what to do next when he heard a rasping sound. He turned in time to see his tauntaun stagger and fall dead to the snow-covered ground.

Temporarily stunned, Han stared at the fallen tauntaun. Then he grabbed Luke's arms and dragged him to the tauntaun's body. "Not much time," he muttered. He knew he'd have to work fast, before the tauntaun's corpse froze.

Luke moaned, "Ben . . . Ben . . ."

Han figured Luke was delirious. "Hang on, kid," he said. He took Luke's lightsaber, ignited its blade, and cut the dead Tauntaun's belly wide open.

"Dagobah system . . ." Luke mumbled. "You will go to Dagobah . . ."

Struggling to get Luke inside the carcass, Han explained, "This may smell bad, kid . . . but it will keep you warm . . . till I can get the shelter built."

Oblivious to everything, Luke moaned, "Yoda . . ."

"Agh!" Han gasped as the gutted beast's rancid stench swam over him. "Agh . . . I thought they smelled bad on the outside! *Agh!*"

With Luke tucked more or less into the tauntaun's body cavity, Han removed a pack and took out a shelter container. The shelter would offer pitiful protection against the bitter cold . . . but it was all Han had.

The next morning offered clear blue skies for the Rebel pilots who raced over Hoth in the four snub-nosed T-47 snowspeeders — enclosed two-man craft that allowed a pilot and gunner to be seated back-to-back. Each of these four carried only a single pilot, to allow room for Luke Skywalker and Han Solo, should either be found. After skirting a high plateau, the snowspeeders veered off in different directions to search for the missing men.

Rebel pilot Zev Senesca's comm-unit designation was Rogue Two. Zev had been on Hoth long enough to have a hard time believing anyone could've survived the previous night's blizzard. Also, the war had claimed too many lives for Zev to be much of an optimist. He was grimly concentrating on the scopes that ringed his cockpit when he heard a low beep from a monitor. Activating his transmitter, he called out, "Echo Base . . . I've got something! Not much, but it could be a life-form. . . ."

Zev banked his craft, made a slow arc, then raced off in a new direction. Switching to a different transmission frequency, he said, "Commander Skywalker, do you copy? This is Rogue Two." No response. "This is Rogue Two. Captain Solo, do you copy?"

"Good morning," Han's voice sounded from a speaker in Zev's cockpit. "Nice of you guys to drop by."

It had been weeks since Zev had felt any reason to smile, but the one that broke out across his face went from ear to ear. "Echo Base . . . this is Rogue Two. I found them. Repeat, I found them." He steered the snowspeeder to follow the source of Han's transmission, and soon sighted Han's emergency shelter. Han stood beside the shelter and waved, safe at last.

Luke wondered, *Am I dead?*

His whole body felt empty, drained of life, yet there was a lightness about him. *I feel like I'm floating. But what's that pressure over my mouth and . . . is something pinching my nose? And what are those whirring noises?* Opening his eyes, he saw blurred lights and rising air bubbles, and thought, *I'm drowning!*

He had emerged from unconsciousness to find himself submerged in a transparent cylindrical tank filled with warm liquid. A breathing mask was strapped over his mouth and a small clamp sealed his nostrils. From Luke's perspective, the tank's shape produced a distorted view of strange figures moving outside. But as his vision adjusted, Luke recognized the figures as 2-1B, an older medical droid that served the Rebel Alliance, and his assistant, the multiarmed droid FX-7. It was FX-7 who was responsible for the whirring sounds.

Luke realized he was in the Echo Base medical center, and that the liquid in the tank was bacta, a synthetic chemical that made wounds heal quickly and left no scars. Luke's last conscious memory was of Ben, appearing before him in the snow. *Who rescued me? And how?*

Then he saw his friends. Leia, Han, Chewbacca, R2-D2, and C-3PO were gathered on the other side of the medical center's window. They waved to him. Still groggy, Luke returned the gesture, then felt his body being lifted out of the tank.

It was time to return to the world.

"Master Luke, sir, it's so good to see you fully functional again," C-3PO said to Luke, who now sat on a bed in the medical center's white-walled recovery room. Leia smiled as R2-D2 rolled up beside Luke's bed and beeped.

"Artoo expresses his relief also," C-3PO translated.

Luke was by no means fully functional. He was tired and sore, and his battered features were nasty evidence of his encounter with the wampa. But he was alive and he would heal.

Behind Luke, the door slid open with a soft hiss, and Han and Chewbacca entered.

Han asked, "How you feeling, kid? You don't look so bad to me. In fact, you look strong enough to pull the ears off a gundark."

Luke grinned. "Thanks to you."

"That's two you owe me, junior," Han said, referring to the Battle of Yavin, when he'd prevented Darth Vader from shooting down Luke's starfighter.

Han swiveled to lean against the foot of Luke's bed and face Leia. "Well, Your Worship, looks like you managed to keep me around for a little while longer."

"I had nothing to do with it," Leia retorted. "General Rieekan thinks it's dangerous for any ships to leave the system until we've activated the energy shield." Indeed, the Rebels had been working round-the-clock on the power generators so the energy shields would be ready when needed.

"That's a good story," Han said. "I think you just can't bear to let a gorgeous guy like me out of your sight."

In bed, Luke grimaced. Han was his friend, but the *Millennium Falcon*'s captain was also so full of himself that he could be unbearable. *How can Han talk to Leia that way? She's a princess! Sometimes I wish he would just keep his mouth shut.*

Coolly glaring at Solo, Leia slowly shook her head and said, "I don't know where you get your delusions, laserbrain."

Chewbacca tilted his head back and produced an amused, gurgling bark.

"Laugh it up, fuzzball," Han said reproachfully. "But you didn't see us alone in the south passage." He moved toward Leia and slinked an arm around her back. "She expressed her true feelings for me."

Stunned, Luke's eyes darted from Han to Leia and back to Han. *Is Han serious? Does Leia really want . . . ?*

"My . . . !" Leia gasped, her temper boiling over. Han eased away from Leia as she released a barrage: "Why, you stuck-up . . . half-witted . . . scruffy-looking . . . *nerf herder!*"

"Who's scruffy-looking?" Han asked, looking genuinely insulted. Then he turned to Luke and said, "I must have hit pretty close to the mark to get her all riled up like that, huh, kid?"

But Luke wouldn't meet Han's gaze. He was too angry. Even the droids sensed the tension in the air.

Leia composed herself, then moved closer to

Luke's bed. Looking at Han, she said, "Why, I guess you don't know everything about women yet." Then she leaned over Luke and kissed him on the lips.

Luke thought, *Huh?*

C-3PO, who had been standing just behind Han, nearly tripped over himself to get a better view. After seeing that Leia and Luke were indeed in an embrace, the baffled droid redirected his gaze from Chewbacca to Han to see their reaction. Chewbacca made a curious whimpering sound. Han did his best to keep his expression relaxed and neutral, as if seeing Leia and Luke interested him only mildly.

The kiss lasted about three seconds.

Leia pulled away from Luke. She looked at Han, who kept his expression neutral as he met her gaze. Then, without any further word, Leia walked to the door and left the room.

Han turned his casual gaze to Luke. Luke put his hands behind his head and leaned back into his bed, trying hard to keep a smug smile from his face. *Well, Han, do you have anything to say now?*

From a loudspeaker, a voice announced, "Headquarters personnel, report to command center."

Han glanced at Chewbacca, who tilted his furry head at the door. Trying not to look relieved at the opportunity to make an exit, Han tapped Luke's arm and said, "Take it easy," then followed Chewbacca out of the room.

Ever polite, C-3PO added, "Excuse us, please," and trotted after R2-D2, leaving Luke alone.

Walking fast, Han arrived first at the command center, followed by Leia, Chewbacca, and the droids. Inside the dim, low-ceilinged room, General Rieekan stood beside Wyron Serper, the center's senior controller, who was seated before a console screen. Seeing Leia, General Rieekan said, "Princess . . . we have a visitor."

The group gathered around the console screen and examined a comm-scan display map of Echo Base and its surrounding areas. On the map, a small, unidentified blip appeared to the north. Rieekan said, "We've picked up something outside the base of zone twelve, moving east."

"It's metal," Serper reported.

"Then it couldn't be one of those creatures," Leia said, referring to the wampas.

"It could be a speeder, one of ours," Han suggested.

Serper raised a hand to adjust a control on his headset. "No," he said. "Wait — there's something very weak coming through." Serper switched on an audio speaker, allowing the others to hear the intercepted transmission, a strange series of choppy electronic noises.

Looking to Rieekan, C-3PO said, "Sir, I am fluent in

six million forms of communication. This signal is not used by the Alliance. It could be an Imperial code."

With that possibility in mind, the gathered Rebels listened even more attentively to the signal. After several seconds, Han decided, "It isn't friendly, whatever it is." Without waiting for the general or anyone else to issue an order, Han turned to his first mate and said, "Come on, Chewie, let's check it out."

As Han and Chewbacca headed for the hangar, Rieekan thought they might require backup. To Serper, Rieekan said, "Send Rogues Ten and Eleven to station three-eight."

Trouble had arrived.

When the Imperial probot was finished sending its message, it retracted its two high-frequency transmission antennae down into its sensor head. Then the droid hovered away from its hiding place behind a wide snowdrift, where its telescopic sensors had maintained an unobstructed view of the Rebels' power generator.

The probot was heading down a ridge toward the Rebel base when its sensors detected movement by a nearby snowbank. The probot spun its sensor head and directed its primary visual sensors at the snowbank, where a Wookiee's snow-covered head had popped up.

Chewbacca ducked as the droid fired three rapid laser bursts. The laser bolts missed the Wookiee and bored into the snowbank.

But Chewbacca was just a decoy, and Han — concealed behind a rise of glacial rock — was right behind the droid. While the droid was still distracted, Han rose and snapped off a quick shot at the droid's hovering form. Unlike the droid, Han didn't miss.

The fired bolt slammed into the droid but barely dented its metal plating. The droid responded by quickly rotating its cylindrical body in midair and firing back at Han. But Han had already ducked and the droid missed again.

Han came up fast and fired a second blast at the droid, again meeting his mark. After the way the droid had taken his first shot, Han knew he'd be lucky if he could disable it. So he was surprised when — a moment after his second shot hit the droid — the droid exploded into smoke and flames, leaving nothing behind but a fine spray of black-metal dust across the snow.

In the command center, General Rieekan stood next to Leia, who sat at a comm console and listened to Han's report. From the comlink, Han's voice said, "'Fraid there's not much left."

"What was it?" Leia asked.

"Droid of some kind," Han answered. "I didn't hit it that hard. It must have had a self-destruct."

"An Imperial probe droid," Leia deduced.

Han said, "It's a good bet the Empire knows we're here."

It had been anything but easy for the Rebels to establish a base on Hoth. But if there were even a slight possibility that the Empire knew the location of Echo Base, no one was safe on the ice planet. With grim resolve, Rieekan said, "We'd better start the evacuation."

CHAPTER 3

Many light-years away from Hoth, five Imperial Star Destroyers and their respective TIE fighter escorts rendezvoused in space. Despite the immense size of each Star Destroyer, all fell under the shadow of an even more enormous ship: the *Super*-class Star Destroyer, *Executor*.

At 8,000 meters long, the *Executor* was the largest traditional starship constructed by the Imperial Navy. Only the Death Star space station had been larger. Equipped with more than a thousand weapons, the *Executor* carried 144 TIE fighters and 38,000 stormtroopers. And all were at the disposal of the ship's commander: Darth Vader, Lord of the Sith.

Clad entirely in black, with a helmet that completely concealed his head and a cape that reached the floor, Darth Vader was darker than deepest space. On the *Executor*'s bridge, he stood before a transparisteel viewport and surveyed his fleet. Because the *Executor* was protected by a powerful shielding force field, the bridge was positioned at the bow — usually the most vulnerable area of a starship — and offered Vader a panoramic view unobstructed by any part of his ship.

Behind Vader, a long walkway extended to the captain's control station. The walkway was without railings, and on either side the floor dropped off to expose the bridge's lower level. There, gray-uniformed Imperial technicians operated their console stations, and tried not to look up to find themselves eye level with Darth Vader's boots.

A door opened near the captain's station, and Vader's two chief officers — the pompous Admiral Ozzel and the younger, powerfully built General Veers — entered the bridge. Like all high-ranking Imperial officers, Ozzel and Veers wore gray uniforms and caps, as well as black leather gloves, belts, and boots. They were approaching the walkway that led to Vader when the *Executor*'s captain called out, "Admiral."

"Yes, Captain?" Ozzel answered, turning with Veers to face Captain Piett, a lean man with eyes that appeared tired from staring at monitors.

"I think we've got something, sir," Piett informed him. "The report is only a fragment from a probe droid in the Hoth system, but it's the best lead we've had."

Unimpressed, Ozzel snapped, "We have thousands of probe droids searching the galaxy. I want proof, not leads!"

But Piett wasn't finished. He added, "The visuals indicate life readings."

"It could mean anything," Ozzel said, growing impatient with Piett. "If we followed up every lead . . ."

"But sir," Piett interrupted, "the Hoth system is supposed to be devoid of human forms."

"You found something?" Darth Vader's deep, mechanically tinged voice rumbled, his black mask looking down at Piett. None of the officers had heard or seen his tall, dark form approach.

"Yes, my lord," said Piett, directing Vader's attention to a lower console monitor. The monitor displayed the transmitted image of a snow-base power generator.

"That's it," Vader said with conviction. "The Rebels are there."

Admiral Ozzel saw nothing on the monitor that specifically indicated a Rebel presence, and he did not believe in expending time and energy on a mere hunch. Employing what he considered his most diplomatic manner, Ozzel still sounded condescending when he spoke: "My lord, there are so many uncharted settlements. It could be smugglers, it could be . . ."

"That is the system," Vader interrupted. His tone was

filled with restrained menace, making it clear that he would not tolerate any questioning of his actions. "Set your course for the Hoth system. General Veers, prepare your men." Darth Vader turned and stalked off the bridge.

Veers looked at Ozzel, who appeared stung by Vader's lack of respect for military protocol. Hoping to restore his commanding officer's confidence, Veers said, "Admiral?"

Ozzel nodded, giving *his* permission for Veers to prepare the soldiers, as if his permission even mattered. Veers walked off quickly, and Ozzel — furious over his treatment by Vader — threw a threatening gaze at Piett before he left in a huff.

If Captain Piett was afraid of Admiral Ozzel, he didn't show it. In Piett's experience, it was smarter to be afraid of Darth Vader.

On Hoth, everyone at Echo Base was preparing to evacuate. In the transport bay, several transports were being loaded by soldiers carrying heavy boxes of equipment and supplies. The soldiers moved quickly, but not in panic. Near one transport, two Rebels faced their captain.

"Groups seven and ten will stay behind to fly the speeders," the captain ordered, prompting one soldier to walk off quickly. Turning to the remaining soldier, the captain said, "As soon as each transport is loaded, evacuation control will give clearance for immediate launch."

"Right, sir," answered the soldier.

In the main hangar deck, Han was atop the *Millennium Falcon*, trying frantically to complete the welding on the lifters. In the *Falcon*'s cockpit, Chewbacca sat ready at the controls. After finishing a weld, Han stood up and shouted, "All right, that's it. Try it . . ."

Chewbacca threw a switch. Unfortunately, the switch accidentally triggered a minor explosion on the problematic lifter, and nearly launched Han from the *Falcon*'s hull.

"Off!" Han shouted as he leaped away from another small explosion. "Turn it off! Turn it off! Off!"

Chewbacca howled as his furry fingers darted from one switch to the next. When he realized Han had stopped shouting, the Wookiee looked from the cockpit to see if he was all right. At first, all he saw was smoke.

The smoke cleared. Han was unhurt but exasperated as he surveyed the new damage. Sometimes, being captain of the fastest ship in the galaxy was not as thrilling as it could be.

In the medical center, Luke got into his bright-orange pressurized g-suit. He was almost ready to leave when 2-1B turned his skull-like metal head in time to see his departing patient. Luke had the impression that 2-1B had genuinely enjoyed hearing about the technical challenges of converting T-47 airspeeders into snowspeeders, and wasn't surprised when the droid commented, "Sir, it will take quite a while to evacuate the T-47s."

"Well, forget the heavy equipment," Luke said. "There's plenty of time to get the smaller modules on the transports." He grabbed his flight gear and headed for the door.

2-1B said, "Take care, sir."

During his recovery, Luke had gotten to observe the droid well enough to know he meant it. Luke smiled and said, "Thanks."

Leaving the medical center, he proceeded through the laser-cut corridors to the main hangar. Pilots, gunners, and astromech droids scurried about as he walked toward Chewbacca, who was now working under the *Millennium Falcon.*

"Chewie, take care of yourself, okay?" Luke said, and reached up to scratch the Wookiee's neck. Luke turned to walk away, but Chewbacca threw his arms around Luke and gave him a tight hug before letting him go. Luke looked up to find Han standing atop the *Falcon* with a small repair droid.

"Hi, kid," Han said from his elevated position, then turned to the repair droid and scolded, "There's got to be a reason for it. Check it at the other end. Wait a second." While the droid rotated its visual sensors, Han looked back down at Luke and asked, "You all right?"

"Yeah," Luke said. There were so many things he wanted to tell Han. How much their friendship meant, how he hoped Han wasn't hurt by Leia's rejection, how he wished him safety and happiness . . . but everything he thought of saying somehow sounded like the one thing he didn't want to say: *Good-bye.* So Luke just nodded, then started to walk away.

"Be careful," Han said.

Glancing back, Luke said, "You, too."

In the command center, a Rebel controller urgently gestured for General Rieekan and reported, "General, there's a fleet of Star Destroyers coming out of hyperspace in sector four."

Rieekan leaned over the controller's shoulder to examine the monitor display of sector four, then ordered, "Reroute all power to the energy shield." Turning from the controller, Rieekan faced a Rebel officer and said, "We've got to hold them till all the transports are away. Prepare for ground assault."

While the *Executor* and five Star Destroyers had traveled through hyperspace to arrive in orbit of the ice planet Hoth, Darth Vader had been inside his meditation chamber. A spherical enclosure with a black exterior, the chamber was pressurized to keep Vader comfortable, even with his helmet off.

General Veers entered Vader's private quarters and carefully approached the chamber. Veers stood at attention as jawlike clamps unlocked at the sphere's side, allowing its upper half to rise.

Darth Vader was seated in the center of the chamber's bright white interior. His black helmet was already facing the general, as if he'd been anticipating this meeting.

"What is it, General?" Vader asked.

"My lord, the fleet has moved out of lightspeed," Veers reported. "Comm-scan has detected an energy field protecting an area of the sixth planet of the Hoth system. The field is strong enough to deflect any bombardment."

Vader seethed. "The Rebels are alerted to our presence. Admiral Ozzel came out of lightspeed too close to the system."

Hoping to explain Admiral Ozzel's decision, Veers said, "He felt surprise was wiser. . . ."

"He is as clumsy as he is stupid," Vader interrupted. "General, prepare your troops for a surface attack."

"Yes, my lord," Veers said, then left.

Vader's seat rotated, allowing him to face a wide

viewscreen. It flicked on and displayed an image of Admiral Ozzel and Captain Piett on the *Executor*'s bridge. Ozzel turned his face and said, "Lord Vader, the fleet has moved out of lightspeed, and we're preparing to — aaagh!"

On the viewscreen, Ozzel was touching his throat with his left hand. Vader, using the Force, had constricted Ozzel's windpipe.

"You have failed me for the last time, Admiral," Vader said.

Admiral Ozzel took a step backward but remained on the viewscreen.

Vader said, "Captain Piett."

"Yes, my lord," said Piett, tearing his eyes away from the choking admiral to face Vader.

"Make ready to land our troops beyond their energy field and deploy the fleet so that nothing gets off the system." As Admiral Ozzel's strangled form fell to the bridge's deck with an audible thud, Vader added, "You are in command now, *Admiral* Piett."

Piett straightened and said, "Thank you, Lord Vader." He looked to some nearby soldiers and jerked his head slightly, silently instructing them to remove Ozzel's corpse. Piett had always strived to learn from the mistakes of others, but he had not expected a promotion so soon.

*   *   *

There was a sense of urgency at Echo Base. No one knew when the Imperials would strike, but everyone was certain that an attack was inevitable. And because the Rebels' energy shield would protect the base from aerial attack, the Rebels knew the assault would come from the ground.

In the center of the main hangar, Princess Leia and Major Derlin briefed a group of pilots. Leia told them, "All troop carriers will assemble at the north entrance. The heavy transport ships will leave as soon as they're loaded. Only two fighter escorts per ship. The energy shield can only be opened for a short time, so you'll have to stay very close to your transports."

"Two fighters against a Star Destroyer?" said a young pilot who everyone called Hobbie. He sounded more than a little doubtful.

Turning to Hobbie, Leia explained, "The ion cannon will fire several shots to make sure that any enemy ships will be out of your flight path. When you've gotten past the energy shield, proceed directly to the rendezvous point." She gestured to all the pilots. "Understand?"

In unison, the pilots replied in the affirmative. Leia knew, despite any doubts, they would do everything they could to make the plan work. "Good luck," she wished them.

"Okay," said Major Derlin, clapping his gloved hands for attention. "Everybody to your stations. Let's go!" The pilots went to their vehicles, and Leia ran to the command center.

Outside the ice cave, Rebel soldiers carried weapons and positioned them along snow trenches, while others loaded power packs into gun turrets. Near the base power generators, troops rushed to set up their heavy battle equipment. And all around Echo Base, Rebel lookouts trained their eyes and macrobinoculars to the surrounding ice plains, scanning for any sign of the anticipated Imperial troops.

Leia arrived in the command center to find General Rieekan with his eyes glued to the comm-scan display. At their consoles, the Rebel controllers were tense, and everyone was trying hard not to show any fear.

Rieekan said, "Their primary target will be the power generators." He turned to a controller and said, "Prepare to open shield."

The Rebels' protective energy shield was opened, allowing two X-wing starfighters to escort a bulky, 90-meter-long transport up and away from Hoth's surface, leaving Echo Base at least temporarily exposed to the Imperials.

Now all the three Rebel ships had to do was get past the hulking Star Destroyers.

CHAPTER 4

As expected, the two X-wings and the Rebel transport did not go unnoticed as they rose quickly through Hoth's atmosphere. On the bridge of one Imperial Star Destroyer, an Imperial controller approached his captain, who was regarding the ice world through the main viewport.

"Sir," said the controller. "Rebel ships are coming into our sector."

"Good," said the captain. "Our first catch of the day."

Inside the Echo Base command center, a female controller kept her eyes on the comm-scan display, watching the three rising blips that indicated the transport and its two X-wing escorts. On their present course, the vessels were heading almost straight for a Star Destroyer.

"Stand by, ion control," the controller said into a

transmitter while she watched the blips. When she knew the Rebel ships were almost within visual range of the destroyer, she gave the command: "Fire!"

Outside the Rebel base, a giant ball-shaped ion cannon made pumping motions as it blasted three consecutive red energy beams skyward. Each energy beam streaked past the escaping Rebel ships and didn't stop until they smashed into the waiting Star Destroyer.

The scarlet bolts took out the destroyer's missile launchers and conning tower, and caused a series of fiery explosions to spread across its metal hull. The destroyer veered, then spun out of control. As the Imperial ship careered into deep space, the Rebel transport and X-wings raced onward to safety.

Back at Echo Station, Rebel pilots, gunners, and ground troops were hurrying to their stations and vehicles when they heard a controller announce over loudspeakers: "The first transport is away." Throughout the base, the Rebels cheered. It was hardly time to celebrate, but the battle had gotten off to a promising start.

In the main hangar, pilots and gunners were scrambling into their snowspeeders, which were lined up in rows with their cockpit canopies raised. When Luke arrived at his speeder, he found his gunner — a fresh-faced, eager kid named Dack Ralter — already in the speeder's aft-facing gunner's seat.

Dack turned his head to see Luke and asked, "Feeling all right, sir?"

"Just like new, Dack," Luke said as he climbed into the pilot's seat. "How about you?"

"Right now I feel like I could take on the whole Empire myself."

Luke grinned. "I know what you mean." He pulled on his helmet as Dack lowered the cockpit canopy. With the canopy in place, Luke glanced through its transparisteel windows to look at the other pilots of Rogue Group, who would be under his command. The pilots included Zev Senesca, who'd been first to locate Han and Luke after their long night out in the snow; Wedge Antilles, who'd also seen combat at the Battle of Yavin; and Hobbie, who'd known Luke's friend Biggs Darklighter.

Luke hoped all the Rebel pilots would survive the day.

Outside the hangar, hundreds of Rebel troops took up their positions in a series of long snow trenches. There was a tense silence among the soldiers as they braced their blaster rifles along the upper banks of the trenches and gazed out over the bleak landscape, watching the horizon for any movement.

They didn't have to wait long. Small dot-sized objects began to appear on the horizon. The dots were moving in the direction of the Rebel base.

A Rebel officer lifted a pair of macrobinoculars to

his eyes. Through the lens, he saw a very close view of a giant battle machine that traveled on four long, jointed legs. He adjusted the view to zoom back and saw three more of the armored behemoths. The trench officer had no difficulty identifying the machines as Imperial AT-ATs: All Terrain Armored Transports.

At 20 meters long and over 15 meters tall, AT-ATs were heavily armored and almost unstoppable weapons platforms. Although the AT-ATs resembled robot quadrupeds, they were manned vehicles, operated from within the command section that extended from the front like a head, and had the capacity to carry up to forty troopers. Each AT-AT command section was armed with two side-mounted medium blaster cannons and two heavy laser cannons that jutted out from under the command section's "chin."

The AT-ATs were still distant, but the rhythmic pounding of their lumbering footsteps was already causing the ground to vibrate at Echo Base. The trench officer lowered his macrobinoculars and spoke into his comlink: "Echo Station Three-t-eight. We have spotted Imperial walkers!"

Back at the command center, the trench officer's report was received and relayed by a controller: "Imperial walkers on the north ridge."

The snowspeeder pilots responded immediately. The speeders lifted from the hangar floor, raced out of the cave, and flew above the ice field at full throt-tle. Accelerating away from the base, they headed toward the distant Imperial walkers.

From the trenches, there were now five walkers vis-ible. The lead walker did not pause its advance as it opened fire, blasting red energy beams at the Rebel troops. Fire and ice exploded around the trenches, sending the Rebels diving for cover.

Flying past a Rebel battlement, Luke sighted the walkers and said, "Echo Station Five-seven. We're on our way."

The snowspeeders flew low over trenches, where Rebel troops were now firing at the approaching walkers. Luke addressed the other pilots via his hel-met's comlink: "All right, boys, keep tight now."

The walkers' heads were attached to flexible ar-mored necks, and the heads angled to fire at the in-coming snowspeeders. Red energy bolts whizzed past the evasive speeders, but the Rebel pilots kept heading for their targets.

Behind Luke, Dack adjusted his targeting system to aim for the walker's forward laser cannons. Dack warned, "Luke, I have no approach vector. I'm not set."

"Steady, Dack," Luke replied. "Attack pattern delta. Go now."

Luke banked his speeder to the right of one walker, knowing he was trailed by the speeder flown by Hobbie. Then Luke angled back toward the walker and said, "All right, I'm coming in."

As Luke threw his speeder into a steep dive toward the walker's left side, Dack squeezed the triggers for the laser cannons. Luke watched the speeder's cannons fire and score several direct hits, all ineffective, then steered the speeder between the walker's left legs and under the machine's belly. He pulled back on his flight controls to bring the speeder into a rapid ascent over another walker, and Dack fired at that walker, too, without making a dent.

Luke shouted into his comlink, "Hobbie, you still with me?"

Hobbie was, and kept his speeder close on Luke's wing. The two speeders raced directly at the head of a walker, fired their cannons, then split and flew past it. From his aerial position, Luke made a quick survey of the battle below and all around him. A speeder banked through and away from the legs of a walker, then the walker swiveled and fired, striking a snowspeeder and sending it crashing into the snow.

Luke looked back at the walker and said, "That armor's too strong for blasters."

On the horizon, another walker moved up past Luke's cockpit window. Luke banked and began to make another run. Into his comlink, he said, "Rogue Group, use your harpoons and tow cables. Go for the legs. It might be our only chance of stopping them." Luke guided the speeder straight for the walker and said, "All right, stand by, Dack."

"Oh, Luke, we've got a malfunction in fire control," Dack reported with concern. "I'll have to cut in the auxiliary."

"Just hang on," Luke said. He wished he could see what Dack was doing, but the cockpit's back-to-back seating made that virtually impossible. Keeping his eyes focused on the walker, Luke assured his gunner again, "Hang on, Dack. Get ready to fire that tow cable."

Energy bolts streaked from the walker and exploded in midair bursts, creating a deadly obstacle course for Luke. The flak buffeted the snowspeeder. Dack was struggling to set up his harpoon gun when Luke heard an explosion from behind.

"Dack?" Luke said. When no answer came, he repeated louder, "Dack!"

But Dack was lost, his body slumped over his smoldering controls.

General Veers stood at his station inside the command section of the lead AT-AT. In front of him, two pilots sat behind their controls and faced a wide, viewport. Through the thin viewport, Veers saw a Rebel speeder bank in from the side and head straight at the command section. The speeder's cannons fired, blasting away at the AT-AT's viewport. An explosion rippled across the walker's windows, then quickly dissipated, causing no damage.

Veers guided his impregnable war machine closer to a line of trenches and fired the AT-AT's laser cannons. A Rebel gun turret was hit and exploded. A handful of Rebels held their ground and returned fire, for all the good it did them, while the rest scattered away from the burning turret.

When the smoke cleared, Veer and his pilots sighted the Rebel power generators in the distance. Once the generators were destroyed, the energy shield would be down and the Rebels would be completely vulnerable. However, Veers's AT-AT was not yet within firing range.

Veers's command console was equipped with a compact HoloNet transceiver, which could transmit and project holograms: three-dimensional images produced by beams of light. The shallow bowl-shaped transceiver activated to display a flickering blue hologram of Darth Vader.

"Yes, Lord Vader," Veers addressed the holographic image. "I've reached the main power generators. The shield will be down in moments. You may start your landing."

*   *   *

Luke knew there was nothing he could do about Dack. He also knew he had to keep flying and not leave the fight, doing whatever he could to stop the Imperial walkers. If he couldn't launch his speeder's harpoon and tow cable, then he'd help another pilot execute the plan.

Luke spotted a snowspeeder flying off his port wing. It was Wedge. Into his comlink, Luke said, "Rogue Three."

"Copy, Rogue Leader," Wedge answered from his speeder.

"Wedge, I've lost my gunner," Luke said as he angled back to the walker. "You'll have to make this shot. I'll cover for you." Luke began a wide sweep around the walker and instructed, "Set your harpoon. Follow me on the next pass."

"Coming around, Rogue Leader," Wedge replied, steering after Luke. Behind Wedge sat his gunner, Wes Janson. With steely nerves, Janson readied his harpoon gun.

Trying to distract the walker's crew, Luke flew past the command section's viewport. As more flak exploded around his speeder, he glanced from his cockpit to see Wedge fly his own speeder under the same walker. "Steady, Rogue Two," Luke warned another pilot.

Wedge's speeder had barely passed under the

walker's belly when Wedge ordered: "Activate harpoon."

Janson pressed the firing switch, and the harpoon launched. The harpoon — tipped with a fusion disk that would adhere to any metal surface — flew straight at one of the walker's ankles and embedded itself. As Wedge banked hard to the left, Janson could see a thin line of the retractable flexisteel tow cable trailing behind them.

"Good shot, Janson," Wedge said. He continued banking until he circled the walker, wrapping the tow cable around the Imperial machine's enormous legs. Janson clung to the harpoon gun and watched the tow cable. If Janson didn't detach the cable at just the right time . . . Wedge didn't even want to think about it.

"One more pass," Wedge said as he banked around the front of the walker.

"Coming around," Janson said. "Once more."

Wedge swung the speeder between the legs of the giant walker, and Janson shouted, "Cable out! Let her go!"

"Detach cable," Wedge ordered.

Janson pressed a switch, and the cable release on the back of the speeder snapped loose. As the cable dropped away, Janson said, "Cable detached."

Wedge accelerated away from the walker. The enormous war machine attempted to step forward, but the cable had so thoroughly tangled its legs that it began to topple. It teetered for a moment, then crashed heavily onto the icy ground.

In the trenches, the Rebel troops cheered at the sight of the fallen walker. A trench officer shouted, "Come on!"

But it wasn't necessary for the ground troops to charge the downed walker. From overhead, Wedge and another Rebel pilot descended in their speeders and fired energy charges at their Imperial target. At least one of the charges penetrated the AT-AT's armor plating, for in the next moment, the entire walker was consumed in a massive explosion, launching bits of metal in all directions.

From his cockpit, Wedge shouted, "Woo-ha! That got him!"

"I see it, Wedge," Luke said, watching the spectacle from his own speeder. "Good work."

The battle was taking its toll on the Rebels' command center, where large chunks of ice tumbled from the walls and ceiling. C-3PO stood nervously beside Princess Leia in front of a comm-scan display as another shock wave rocked the room.

General Rieekan approached Leia and said, "I don't think we can protect two transports at a time."

"It's risky," Leia admitted, "but we can't hold out much longer. We have no choice."

With reluctance, Rieekan ordered, "Launch patrols."

Leia turned to an aide and said, "Evacuate remaining ground staff."

Hearing this, C-3PO did not bother to excuse himself as he exited the command center. He knew every detail of the evacuation plan, including R2-D2's assignment. R2-D2 was to guide Luke's X-wing starfighter out of the hangar through the south entrance of Echo Base, then meet Luke on the slope near the ion cannon. C-3PO walked quickly through the laser-cut corridor, hoping he'd be able to say good-bye to his friend before he left the hangar.

As the golden droid entered the hangar, he saw many Rebel soldiers running to their ships. He was walking toward Luke's X-wing when he overheard Han Solo shouting, "No, no! No!"

C-3PO glanced up to see Chewbacca atop the *Millennium Falcon*, sitting half in the starboard mandible's maintenance access bay. Apparently, the *Falcon*'s repairs were not yet finished. Then C-3PO saw Han appear next to Chewbacca. Han gestured with his hand into the access bay and snarled, "This one goes there, that one goes there. Right?"

C-3PO walked past the *Falcon* until he arrived at Luke's X-wing, just in time. A tubular hoist was secured to R2-D2's dome, and a technician was already raising the plucky astromech from the floor.

"Artoo, you take good care of Master Luke now, understand?" C-3PO said. R2-D2 answered with affirmative beeps and whistles as the technician guided and lowered his cylindrical body into the X-wing's astromech socket, just behind the cockpit. C-3PO added, "And . . . do take good care of yourself."

R2-D2 replied with another round of beeps.

C-3PO shook his head and walked away from the X-wing. "Oh, dear, oh, dear," he said as he headed back to the command center.

On the vast snow plains of Hoth, the battle raged on. The Imperial walkers fired lasers as they lumbered onward and continued their slow, steady assault on the Rebel base. Another Rebel gun tower was destroyed, then another, and another.

Inside his own AT-AT's command section, General Veers studied various readouts on his control console. His AT-AT was almost near firing range of the Rebels' generator. Veers turned to a white-armored Imperial snowtrooper and said, "All troops will debark for ground assault." Then Veers turned back to the AT-AT's two pilots and said, "Prepare to target the main generator."

Flak burst around Luke's snowspeeder as it hurtled through the cold skies of Hoth. Glancing to a speeder that was traveling through the air to his left, he sighted Zev in the cockpit. Into his comlink, Luke asked, "Rogue Two, are you all right?"

"Yeah," Zev replied. In fact, there was some blood on Zev's face, but the brave pilot was still alert. "I'm with you, Rogue Leader."

"We'll set harpoon," Luke said. "I'll cover for you."

Luke and Zev raced their speeders toward the giant walkers. As Zev prepared for the attack he said, "Coming around."

The Imperial walkers fired red laser bolts that streaked past the snowspeeders. Cautioning his fellow pilots, Luke said into his comlink, "Watch that cross fire, boys."

Zev said, "Set for position three." He angled his speeder for the harpoon tactic, then said to his gunner, "Steady."

Luke flew fast alongside Zev and warned him to stay tight and low.

Suddenly, Zev's speeder was hit by a laser bolt. Zev yelled as his ship bucked violently, then his cockpit exploded and his flaming speeder fell from the sky.

Luke was flying through flak. He tried to stabilize, but then there was a sound like a thunderclap as an explosion rocked his speeder. The noise caused Luke to reflexively close his eyes. When he opened them, there was a nasty crack across his cockpit window. His speeder was filling with smoke, and electrical sparks rippled over his controls. Luke shouted into the comlink, "Hobbie, I've been hit!"

Smoke poured out of the back of Luke's speeder. He gripped the controls and struggled with them, but they were useless. As he hurtled faster toward the oncoming Imperial walker, he knew he was going to crash.

CHAPTER 5

Luke braced himself as his speeder — now totally out of control — veered to the right of the oncoming Imperial walker and went down. Fortunately, the snow was deep where the speeder crashed — but he still landed hard, and felt the safety harness dig into his torso before he came to a dead stop.

Thick black smoke billowed from the snowspeeder's main thrusters. Luke pushed up the speeder's damaged canopy in time to see another walker advancing toward him. He slipped out of his harness, turned to the backseat, and grabbed hold of Dack's shoulder. He'd hoped to haul his gunner's body out of the cockpit, but when he glanced again at the walker, he knew he'd never make it.

Then he looked to a slot beside his seat:

EMERGENCY SURVIVAL STORAGE.

Still in the cockpit, Luke risked another glance at

the approaching walker, which would be on top of him in one more step. Desperately reaching into the storage slot, he grabbed two items, then threw his body out of the cockpit just as one of the walker's massive footpads came crashing down on his ruined snowspeeder.

Luke clutched the two items he'd hastily selected. One was a portable harpoon gun. The other was a concussion charge.

Luke started running after the Imperial walker.

Han Solo dodged broken steam pipes and crumbling ice ceilings as he raced through the underground corridors from the hangar to the Echo Base command center. When he burst into the command center, it was a shambles, but he was not surprised that a few people remained at their posts. He spotted C-3PO, then saw Leia just beyond the golden droid. She was at one of the control consoles, standing beside a seated controller, still trying to help others.

Han shouted, "You all right?"

C-3PO looked in Han's direction. Leia nodded and yelled back, "Why are you still here?"

"I heard the command center had been hit."

C-3PO turned to Leia to hear her response, which was: "You got your clearance to leave." She returned her attention to the console. C-3PO looked back at Han.

"Don't worry, I'll leave," Han said. "First I'm going to get you to your ship."

"Your Highness," C-3PO pleaded, "we must take this last transport. It's our only hope."

Brushing past debris that had fallen in the middle of the command center, Leia went to another controller and said, "Send all troops in sector twelve to the south slope to protect the fighters." She thought, *That'll give Luke and the other pilots a better chance of reaching their ships.*

Just then, a blast rocked the command center, and C-3PO was thrown backward into Han's arms. Over a loudspeaker, a controller announced, "Imperial troops have entered the base. Imperial troops have entered —"

Han righted C-3PO, then stepped over to Leia, grasped her upper arm, and said, "Come on . . . that's it."

Leia held Han's gaze for a moment before the realization hit her: *We've lost the base.* She then turned back to the seated controller and said, "Give the evacuation code signal. And get to your transports!"

Into a comlink, the controller said, "K-one-zero . . . all troops disengage."

Han could see Leia was exhausted. Keeping his grip on her arm, he started to lead her out of the command center to the corridor. Behind them, C-3PO cried, "Oh! Wait for me!"

*　　*　　*

Back in the trenches, the situation had become dire.

"Begin retreat!" shouted the Rebel trench officer.

A second officer commanded, "Fall back! Fall back!"

The troops responded, fleeing from the battle as the snow-covered ground exploded around them. The Imperial walkers fired their lasers at the running Rebels, continuing their advance toward Echo Base.

But Luke — still on the battlefield — wasn't ready to retreat. The way he saw things, the Rebel soldiers would have a better chance of making it to their transports if he could bring down one more Imperial walker.

Luke watched a nearby walker's foot rise, then ran under it. He fired his harpoon gun at the walker's underside, and a thin cable trailed after the rising, fusion-tipped projectile. The harpoon struck the metal hull and attached firmly.

Still running, Luke clipped the harpoon gun's cable drum to his belt buckle. Instantly, his feet left the ground and he was pulled up by the cable until he came to a stop just under the walker's lower plating.

Hanging precariously near a solid metal hatch, Luke reached to his utility belt for his lightsaber and activated its blade. In a swift motion, he cut through the hatch, then deactivated his lightsaber and returned it to his belt, where he'd also attached the concussion charge. Snapping the concussion charge from his belt, he hurled it up through the open hatch, then released his belt clip from the cable drum.

Luke plunged and landed hard, facedown. Fortunately, the deep snow broke most of his fall. The Imperial walker continued forward and one of its rear footpads nearly struck Luke. Then the walker stopped mid-step, and a muffled explosion came from within. Luke raised his head in time to watch the AT-AT's body rupture, blasting black smoke from its seams and every narrow opening. The smoldering behemoth teetered, then became the second Imperial walker to fall on Hoth.

General Veers saw the second AT-AT fall, then guided his own walker past its burning bulk. Without taking his eyes from the viewport, he addressed the pilot to his right: "Distance to power generators?"

"One-seven, decimal two-eight," the pilot answered.

A Rebel snowspeeder flew into Veers's path, and Veers took over the weapons controls to angle his walker's cannons, then fired. The blast slapped the speeder out of the sky and sent it into a spiral that ended with a fiery explosion in the snow.

Veers reached for the electrorangefinder and lined up the main generator. "Target," he said. "Maximum firepower."

The AT-AT spat out energy beams from its laser cannons, and blew the generator sky high.

With C-3PO several paces behind them, Han and Leia were running through an ice corridor, heading for Leia's transport, when the power generator exploded. They didn't actually see the explosion, but from the muffled roar that echoed throughout the base, they knew something big had blown up. As Han and Leia rounded a corner, the corridor's ice walls buckled and large chunks of ice fell from the ceiling, directly in their path.

Han threw himself at Leia, becoming a human shield as he knocked her to the corridor floor. Snow fell and filled the space, covering them with icy dust. Leia remained on the floor while Han rose quickly to find that the route to Leia's transport was now blocked by the cave-in.

Han pulled a comlink from a pocket on his jacket and said, "Transport, this is Solo. Better take off — I can't get to you. I'll get her out on the *Falcon*." He took Leia's arm and urged, "Come on!" as he pulled her up from the floor. Together they hurried back in the other direction —

— and nearly ran straight into C-3PO. The protocol droid had been far enough behind them that he had not seen the cave-in. As Leia and Han bolted past him, C-3PO turned and stammered, "But . . . but . . . but . . . where are you going?" They neither stopped nor answered, so C-3PO ran after them and called, "Oh . . . come back!"

The white-armored Imperial snowtroopers had to blast through the ice and a collapsed doorway to gain entrance to the command center. Two snowtroopers stepped past the broken remains of the tactical screens and comm consoles, and were followed by the dark, menacing form of Darth Vader.

Vader had arrived on Hoth in his personal shuttle. As snowtroopers swarmed into the command center, he paused to survey the shattered machinery, searching for anything that might tell him more about the Rebel insurgency.

"Wait!" C-3PO wailed as he ran after Leia and Han. "Wait for me! Wait! Stop!" The two humans ran through an open doorway, but as the droid followed, the door slid shut in his face. "How typical," C-3PO fumed at the closed door.

Before he could complain further, however, the door slid open and Han seized the droid. "Come on," Han said as he yanked C-3PO after him.

They ran through the cavernous hangar, making their way past abandoned cargo containers until they saw the *Millennium Falcon*. Chewbacca stood at the base of the *Falcon*'s landing ramp and waved his arms urgently at the running figures. But the engines still weren't fired up, so the Wookiee — not wanting to waste any precious seconds — didn't bother waiting at the ramp.

C-3PO ran as fast as he could. Han turned and shouted, "Hurry up, Goldenrod, or you're going to be a permanent resident!"

"Wait! Wait!" the droid cried as he followed Han and Leia up the landing ramp. He was halfway up when he felt the ramp start to rise from the hangar floor, nearly sending him sprawling into the ship.

The hangar was filled with a tortured, whirring sound of the *Falcon*'s engines. Inside the ship's main hold, Han stood before a control panel, flipping switches, while Chewbacca kept his blue eyes on a troublesome gauge. Leia watched as the Wookiee was suddenly struck by an unexpected blast of steam. Han flipped a different switch and said, "How's this?"

Leia gaped at Solo and said, "Would it help if I got out and pushed?"

C-3PO interrupted to say, "Captain Solo, Captain Solo —"

Ignoring the droid, Han answered Leia: "It might."

Still trying to get Han's attention, C-3PO said, "Sir, might I suggest that you —"

Han cut off the droid with a devastating glare. Quickly but reluctantly, C-3PO said, "It can wait."

Leia followed Han as he ran from the hold to the cockpit, where she watched him attempt to activate the cockpit's instruments. The instrument lights came on briefly, then dimmed. Angered and frustrated with his ship's temperamental technology, Han raised a fist and gave the instrument panel a solid whack. The lights illuminated again and stayed on.

Behind Han, Leia watched in disbelief and said, "This bucket of bolts is never going to get us past that blockade."

"This baby's got a few surprises left in her, sweetheart," Han promised as his hands darted across the switches and buttons on the cockpit's instrument panels.

Through the cockpit's transparisteel windows, they saw a squad of Imperial snowtroopers enter the hangar. Most wielded standard-issue blaster rifles, but one team carried a heavy repeating blaster cannon and a tripod. Leia guessed the snowtroopers would have their cannon set up in less than a minute, and she had a hard time believing the *Falcon* would be out of the hangar that soon.

Fortunately, one of the *Falcon*'s surprises was still functioning: An autoblaster — concealed above a panel in the ship's lower hull — popped out of its recess and swiveled to aim at the snowtroopers. The autoblaster spat out a rapid series of laser bolts, cutting down the nearest snowtroopers.

Han slid into the pilot's seat. Behind him, Leia got into the navigator's seat. She felt a thumping vibration as Chewbacca approached, his large feet pounding up the tubular corridor that led to the cockpit.

"Come on! Come on!" Han shouted to the Wookiee, who ducked as he hurried through the cockpit's open hatch. The hatch door slid shut and Chewbacca scrambled into the copilot's seat to Han's right. "Switch over," Han said, ready to give the ignition another try. "Let's hope we don't have burnout."

A blaster bolt struck and glanced off the window near Chewbacca and he let out a nervous yelp. Through the cockpit's window, they saw the snowtroopers had almost completed their assembly of the tripod-mounted cannon. Unlike the Imperial blaster rifles, the cannon had enough firepower to punch holes in the *Falcon*'s hull.

The *Falcon*'s engines fired. Han flashed a grin at Leia and said, "See?"

Not impressed, Leia leaned forward in her seat and said, "Someday you're going to be wrong, and I just hope I'm there to see it."

The snowtroopers were about to fire their cannon when the *Falcon*'s autoblaster swiveled again and unleashed a steady stream of laser fire. The energized projectiles smashed into the cannon, and the

Imperial weapon blew up, throwing the snowtroopers in all directions.

"Punch it!" Han ordered, and Chewie hit the accelerator. Han, Chewbacca, and Leia sank back against their seats as the ship launched forward.

Darth Vader arrived in the hangar just in time to see the *Millennium Falcon* soar out the mouth of the cave and vanish into the sky.

CHAPTER 6

On the south slope outside Echo Base, Luke was making his way to his waiting X-wing starfighter when he heard the sound of a familiar starship's engine. He looked back to see the *Millennium Falcon* race away from the base and travel over the snow, then angle up and away from Hoth's surface.

Luke arrived at the evacuation site as the last Rebel transport was lifting off and the surviving pilots were running to their X-wings. Luke sighted his own X-wing, with R2-D2's blue-domed head poking up from the ship's astromech socket.

"Artoo!" Luke shouted.

Rotating his visual sensors to see Luke, R2-D2 let out some happy beeps.

"Get her ready for takeoff," Luke said. He watched as R2-D2 initiated the X-wing's repulsorlift, opened the cockpit canopy, and guided the vessel over the snow to Luke. As Luke stepped up to the X-wing, he saw Wedge heading for another X-wing.

"Good luck, Luke," Wedge said. "See you at the rendezvous."

R2-D2 made a long whimpering beep as Luke climbed into the cockpit and lowered its canopy. "Don't worry, Artoo," Luke said. "We're going, we're going."

The X-wing ascended through Hoth's atmosphere and Luke kept his eyes open for Imperial ships. But as he entered space, he was surprised not to see even one of the Star Destroyers that had brought the Imperial soldiers to Hoth. He supposed it was possible the destroyers were on the other side of Hoth, beyond his visual range. And he hoped that the Rebel transports and the *Millennium Falcon* had also escaped Hoth without difficulty.

The X-wing was cruising at sublight speed when Luke began to flip a series of control switches. Then he guided the starfighter into a steep turn and continued flying in a different direction.

R2-D2 beeped, and Luke glanced down at a monitor screen on his control panel. On the screen, R2-D2's beep was neatly translated into a text-format question. Luke read the question and replied into his comlink, "There's nothing wrong, Artoo. Just setting a new course."

R2-D2 beeped again, and Luke's monitor displayed another question.

Luke answered, "We're not going to regroup with the others."

R2-D2 whistled in protest.

Luke continued, "We're going to the Dagobah system."

R2-D2 was quiet while Luke checked his readouts and made a few adjustments. In the cockpit, the only sound was the soft hum of the instruments until R2-D2 finally chirped up.

Luke said, "Yes, Artoo?"

R2-D2 uttered a carefully phrased stream of beeps and whistles.

Luke read the translation on his monitor and chuckled. "That's all right. I'd like to keep it on manual control for a while."

The astromech droid let out a defeated whimper. Luke smiled and continued on his course for Dagobah.

The *Millennium Falcon* was not leaving Hoth so easily. The moment the ship entered space, it had four small TIE fighters and one enormous Star Destroyer on its tail. Green laser fire streaked from the TIE fighters, hammering the *Falcon*'s shields.

Inside the *Falcon*'s cockpit, Chewbacca checked a

monitor to confirm the status of the deflector shields, which were taking a pounding from the flak that exploded around the ship. The Wookiee let out a loud howl.

Han answered, "I saw 'em! I saw 'em!"

"Saw what?" Leia said from the seat behind.

"Star Destroyers," Han explained. "Two of them, coming right at us."

Leia spotted the Star Destroyers as the door behind her slid open and C-3PO stumbled into the cockpit. "Sir, sir!" C-3PO called to Han. "Might I suggest —"

"Shut him up or shut him down!" Han snapped at Leia, and C-3PO was pushed to the rear of the cockpit. To Chewbacca, Han shouted, "Check the deflector shields!"

Chewbacca readjusted an overhead switch and barked a reply that didn't sound good.

"Oh, great," Han said. "Well, we can still outmaneuver them."

Han increased power to the thrusters. With one Star Destroyer still directly behind it, the *Millennium Falcon* headed straight for the two oncoming destroyers. When the *Falcon* was practically between the two vessels, he threw his ship into a steep dive. The Star Destroyer that had been behind him was too unwieldy to follow his maneuver, and continued to travel on a collision course with the other Star Destroyers.

Alarms sounded within the three Star Destroyers. Inside one destroyer, an Imperial officer shouted, "Take evasive action!" But it was too late for the two of them. As their hulls made brushing contact, the ugly sound of shredding metal could be heard on the bridges of both ships.

With four TIE fighters still in hot pursuit, the *Millennium Falcon* raced away from the colliding destroyers. Inside the *Falcon*'s cockpit, Leia hung on to her seat and C-3PO braced himself against the hatch as Han and Chewbacca guided their ship through a dizzying spiral to evade the laser-firing TIE fighters.

To Chewbacca, Han shouted, "Prepare to make the jump to lightspeed!"

"But sir!" C-3PO cried to no avail. Han was already reaching for the hyperdrive controls.

Leia saw the TIE fighters appear as incoming blips on a monitor and shouted, "They're getting closer!"

"Oh, yeah?" Han said with a gleam in his eye. "Watch this." He pulled back on the hyperdrive shift. All eyes looked forward through the cockpit's windows, to the starfield beyond. Han waited for his ship to hurtle forward into hyperspace and transform the view into long streaks of starlight . . . but out-side the cockpit, the distant stars remained fixed against the darkness of space.

"Watch what?" Leia asked.

Han examined the controls and muttered, "I think we're in trouble."

"If I may say so, sir," C-3PO said, "I noticed ear-lier, the hyperdrive motivator has been damaged. It's impossible to go to lightspeed!"

"We're in trouble!" Han decided as he switched to autopilot and rose from his seat. Chewbacca fol-lowed Han out of the cockpit and ran to the hold, where the mighty Wookiee bent to the deck and raised a metal plate to reveal a systems access area: a pit filled with a complex tangle of metal pipes, ca-bles, and wires. Han hastily lowered himself into the pit while Chewbacca turned his attention to a nearby systems monitor panel.

In the pit, Han wrapped his body around a hori-zontally stretched pipe and reached out to adjust a cir-cuit switch. He shouted, "Horizontal boosters . . . !"

From the far side of the hold, Chewbacca an-swered with a loud, negative bark.

Han twisted his body around the metal pipe to reach for some different switches. He shouted, "Allu-vial dampers! Now?" Another negative bark came from Chewbacca. Han said, "That's not it."

A moment later, Chewbacca heard Han call from

the pit: "Bring me the hydrospanners!" The Wookiee picked up a toolbox that had been resting on top of a metal barrel, then shuffled across the deck and placed the toolbox at the edge of the open pit. Han climbed up to select a hydrospanner from the toolbox and said, "I don't know how we're going to get out of this one." He had just lowered himself from Chewbacca's view when the *Falcon* was struck by something that caused a bone-jarring jolt, sending the toolbox sliding into the pit.

"Oww!" Han yelled as the toolbox landed on him. "Chewie!" Han raised himself half out of the pit and felt another jolt, accompanied by a rumbling noise. "Those were no laserblasts!" Han realized. "Something hit us."

As Han scrambled out of the pit, Leia's voice called from a comlink, "Han, get up here!"

"Come on, Chewie!" Han said, racing from the hold.

As Han and Chewbacca rushed into the cockpit, Leia greeted them with a single word: "Asteroids!" Her statement was confirmed by the nightmarish view outside the cockpit window. The *Falcon* had accidentally traveled into the Hoth system's asteroid belt, and thousands of asteroids — pieces of stray matter and planetary debris — drifted through space. Some were small chunks of rock, but others were many times larger than the *Falcon*. Even worse, many asteroids were drifting at different speeds and trajectories.

"Oh, no," Han mumbled. He and Chewbacca pushed their way past Leia and C-3PO to jump back into their respective seats. Solo quickly glanced at the sensor monitors. So far, the *Falcon's* particle shields were holding up against the debris, but the four TIE fighters and a single Star Destroyer were coming up fast behind them. As if to remind Han of their presence, the TIE fighters fired their cannons, and flak buffeted the *Falcon's* shields.

Without hesitation, Han said, "Chewie, set two-seven-one."

The *Millennium Falcon* accelerated, temporarily increasing the distance from the pursuing TIE fighters. But through the *Falcon's* cockpit window, asteroids that were already too close for comfort appeared to grow larger.

"What are you doing?" Leia said to Han. "You're not actually going into an asteroid field?"

"They'd be crazy to follow us, wouldn't they?" Han pointed out, guiding his ship past more asteroids and deeper into the field.

"You don't have to do this to impress me," Leia said, tightening her grip on her seat. She expected Han to respond with some cocky comment, and was dismayed when he didn't. He kept his hands on the controls and his eyes on the sickening view in front of him.

Protocol droids were not programmed to panic, but as C-3PO looked at the asteroids in the *Falcon*'s path, the feeling came to him naturally. Addressing Han, he said, "Sir, the possibility of successfully navigating an asteroid field is approximately three thousand seven hundred and twenty to one."

"Never tell me the odds!" Han said with bravado.

A large asteroid whizzed past the cockpit, then another flew past from a different direction. Han made the *Falcon* drop and weave to avoid being hit. Just off his starboard side, several small asteroids crashed into a larger one. The so-called asteroid field was more like an all-out asteroid storm.

The *Falcon* veered around the large asteroid and raced past the explosion of smaller rocks. The four pursuing TIE fighters tried to swerve around the rocks, but one TIE fighter swooped straight into an asteroid and exploded.

Two huge asteroids tumbled toward the *Millennium Falcon*, which quickly banked around both of them. The three TIE fighters followed but one of them scraped an asteroid and went tumbling out of control and smashed into another asteroid.

Leia risked a glance at one of Han's sensor screens. She saw there were only two TIE fighters still after them, but the pursuing destroyer had also entered the asteroid field. Before she could take any comfort in knowing that the Star Destroyer must be taking a severe beating, she became more concerned with the new bunch of asteroids that appeared to be racing toward the cockpit.

She sat stone-faced, staring through the window as an enormous asteroid dropped past the cockpit and narrowly missed the *Falcon*. Chewbacca barked in terror. C-3PO's hands covered his eyes.

Han gave Leia a quick look. "You said you wanted to be around when I made a mistake; well, this could be it, sweetheart."

"I take it back," Leia gasped. More asteroids raced past the cockpit. "We're going to get pulverized if we stay out here much longer."

"I'm not going to argue with that," Han said.

"Pulverized?" C-3PO repeated, too afraid to process the word.

Han said, "I'm going closer to one of those big ones."

"Closer?" Leia cried in astonishment.

"Closer?" C-3PO echoed.

Louder than Leia and C-3PO, Chewbacca barked the word in his own language.

Han threw the *Millennium Falcon* into a steep dive, aiming toward a moon-sized asteroid. The two remaining TIE fighters followed, and the Imperial pilots fired at the *Falcon* every chance they had.

Seconds later, the *Falcon* was flying dangerously fast and low over the asteroid's crater-pitted surface. Suddenly, the terrain dropped off to reveal a wide, high-walled canyon. As the TIE fighters continued to spit green laser fire after the *Falcon*, Han spotted a jagged, vertical shadow at the far end of the canyon that suggested a ravine between two high cliffs. Without any warning or explanation to his friends, Han raced for the gap. The TIE fighters kept after him.

The *Falcon* sped into the ravine, but the distance between the two cliff walls narrowed rapidly. Banking hard past jagged rock, Han swiftly elevated his ship's port side while dropping the starboard, effectively transforming the *Falcon*'s profile so its height became its width, and allowing the *Falcon* to fly sideways through the ravine.

Although the two TIE fighters were smaller than the *Falcon*, their pilots weren't nearly as skilled as Han Solo. In quick succession, both TIE fighters smashed into the ravine walls and exploded.

Still traveling sideways, the *Millennium Falcon* blasted out of the ravine to emerge in another canyon. As Han stabilized the ship, C-3PO cried, "Oh, this is suicide!"

Han noticed something on his main scope. He

nudged Chewbacca and pointed to a circular shadow on the canyon floor. "There," Han said. "That looks pretty good."

"What looks pretty good?" Leia asked.

"Yeah," Han said. "That'll do nicely."

Baffled, C-3PO turned to Leia and said, "Excuse me, ma'am, but where are we going?"

Out the cockpit window, they saw the same circular shadow: a large crater on the asteroid's surface. Han circled back, then swung the *Falcon* into a dive that deposited them into the crater . . . and total darkness.

At the very tips of the *Falcon*'s extended mandibles, the forward floodlights came on. From what the crew could see, the crater they'd entered was really a deep tunnel.

To Han, Leia said, "I hope you know what you're doing."

All Han could reply was, "Yeah, me too."

CHAPTER 7

Luke Skywalker gazed at the strange, cloud-covered world that now filled the view from his X-wing. Behind him, R2-D2 beeped from his astromech socket, and Luke read R2-D2's words as they were translated on the console monitor.

"Yes, that's it," Luke replied into his comlink. "Dagobah."

R2-D2 beeped a hopeful question.

Luke said, "No, I'm not going to change my mind about this." Examining his sensor scopes, Luke seemed slightly apprehensive. "I'm not picking up any cities or technology. Massive life-form readings though. There's something alive down there. . . ."

Again, R2-D2 beeped, but this time his question was filled with worry.

Luke said, "Yes, I'm sure it's perfectly safe for droids."

It was twilight above Dagobah as Luke began his descent. He entered the atmosphere and his view was soon obscured by clouds. He turned his focus to his sensor scopes . . . and discovered they weren't working.

An alarm began to buzz, and R2-D2 beeped and whistled frantically.

"I know, I know!" Luke said. "All the scopes are dead. I can't see a thing! Just hang on. I'm going to start the landing cycle."

R2-D2 squealed, but his cries were drowned out by the deafening roar of the X-wing's retrorockets. Luke flipped on the landing lights, but he still couldn't see the planet's surface through the dense atmosphere. Suddenly, there was a series of thrashing, cracking sounds, and Luke realized his ship was crashing through the upper branches of tall trees. Then, with a sudden jolt, the X-wing came to a stop.

Luke had landed in a watery peat bog. The X-wing was half-submerged, but from what Luke could see through the fog, his ship was still in one piece.

Luke opened the cockpit canopy and he got his first taste of Dagobah's humid climate. The smell of rot permeated the air. As he pulled off his gloves, he heard the caws and croaks of mysterious, unseen creatures. Behind him, R2-D2 beeped nervously.

Luke climbed out of his cockpit and stepped carefully onto the X-wing's long nose as R2-D2 removed himself from his socket to have a better look at their fog-shrouded surroundings. The X-wing's landing lights barely penetrated the fog, but R2-D2 was able to make out some of the giant, twisted gnarltrees that loomed around them. The gnarltrees had huge roots that rose out of the boggy terrain and gathered into wide trunks. Under and between the roots, cave-sized hollows had formed, leaving natural shelters for creatures of the swamp. Everything appeared to be covered with green moss or slime.

R2-D2 whistled anxiously. Luke turned and said, "No, Artoo, you stay put. I'll have a look around."

Still standing on the X-wing's nose, Luke checked to make sure his blaster was secure in the holster at his right hip, then bent slightly as he removed his helmet. The movement was enough to make his starfighter shift, and R2-D2 was thrown off balance. The droid let out an electronic yelp as he fell into the bog with a loud splash.

Luke spun and called, "Artoo?" He dropped to his knees and leaned out from the X-wing, trying to locate the droid, but the water's surface was blanketed by mist. "Artoo! Where are you? Artoo!" Luke held his breath and waited for some sign of —

A small periscope rose up through the mist. From underwater, R2-D2 made a gurgly beep.

At the sight of the little astromech's periscope, Luke let out a long breath. The periscope rotated so R2-D2 could glimpse his relieved master as he said, "You be more careful."

The periscope began to move through the mist, but Luke saw that R2-D2 wasn't heading in the most direct route to the bog's shore. "Artoo," he said, and the periscope glanced back at him. Luke pointed toward shore and said, "That way!" R2-D2 beeped, then moved off again, following Luke's instruction.

Luke tossed his helmet into the X-wing's open cockpit, then jumped into the murky water. He was right next to the shore and had no difficulty climbing some underwater roots to the muddy ground. But as he emerged with his g-suit covered in muck, he heard R2-D2's pathetic electronic scream.

Luke spun in time to see R2-D2's periscope drop and vanish into the mist, as he caught a glimpse of a large serpentlike creature rolling through the water just behind the droid's position. As suddenly as the creature had revealed its form, it disappeared underwater.

"Artoo!" Luke shouted as he drew his blaster fast, ready to fire at the first sight of the beast when it resurfaced. But seconds passed, and it didn't resurface. Luke watched the mist over the water and waited. *Come on, Artoo. Make a noise. Do something!*

Without warning, there was an explosion of bubbles and mud, and R2-D2 was launched like a missile from the water. Luke watched in stunned silence as the ejected droid sailed through the air, screeching all the way, and dropped out of sight between two trees.

The crash sounded awful.

Luke scrambled over slippery moss and odorous plants to find R2-D2 coated with slime and mud, resting upside down against some gnarled roots.

"Oh, no!" Luke said. "Are you all right?"

R2-D2 beeped and flailed his upturned legs against the vines. Luke noticed some alien bones on the ground nearby, and he wondered if they'd been expectorated by the same creature that had tried to make a meal of R2-D2.

"Come on," Luke said, gently righting the poor droid to his feet. "You're lucky you don't taste very good. Anything broken?"

Nothing appeared to be damaged, but R2-D2 responded with a beep that sounded soggy and miserable.

Luke wiped mud from R2-D2's body. "If you're saying coming here was a bad idea, I'm beginning to agree with you." He stood up and looked around, then squatted down beside the droid. "Artoo, what are we doing here? It's like . . . something out of a dream or . . . I don't know." He pried more mud from the primary photo receptor on R2-D2's domed head and added, "Maybe I'm just going crazy."

R2-D2 beeped, popped open a cranial access port, and spat mud onto the ground.

On the *Executor*, Admiral Piett hesitated as he entered Darth Vader's inner sanctum. From where Piett stood, just at the doorway, he could see Vader's spherical meditation chamber was partially open, but the sphere's interlocking mechanical jaws obscured the view of Vader himself. Piett moved cautiously forward, and when he was able to see the seated figure within the meditation chamber, he gulped in astonishment.

Darth Vader was not wearing his helmet. He sat facing away from Piett, who shivered at the sight of the back of Vader's head; it was pale, hairless, and heavily scarred.

Take a good look, Admiral, thought Vader. *Imagine the worst, and let your fear fuel my power.*

Piett watched a robotic clamp lower from the sphere's ceiling and place the familiar black helmet over Vader's head. He quickly composed himself as Vader's seat rotated to face him.

Vader said, "Yes, Admiral?"

"Our ships have sighted the *Millennium Falcon*, Lord. But . . . it has entered an asteroid field, and we cannot risk —"

"Asteroids do not concern me, Admiral," Vader interrupted. "I want that ship, not excuses."

"Yes, Lord," Piett said as the meditation chamber's upper half descended.

The *Millennium Falcon* had touched down inside the asteroid cave. A sensor scan had detected a warm, pressurized atmosphere outside the ship, but the *Falcon*'s crew was more concerned with repairing their ship than speleological anomalies. Leia, C-3PO, and Chewbacca were checking instruments in the cockpit when Han entered and said, "I'm going to shut down everything but the emergency power systems."

Hearing this, C-3PO said, "Sir, I'm almost afraid to ask, but . . . does that include shutting me down, too?"

"No," Han said with a smile as he flipped several switches to *off* positions. "I need you to talk to the *Falcon* and find out what's wrong with the hyperdrive."

Suddenly, the ship lurched, causing the cockpit's occupants to stumble into one another. A moment after it happened, the ship stabilized.

Facing Han, C-3PO said, "Sir, it's quite possible this asteroid is not entirely stable."

"Not entirely stable?" Han said with annoyance. "I'm glad you're here to tell us these things." He pushed C-3PO toward Chewbacca and said, "Chewie, take the professor in the back and plug him into the hyperdrive."

"Oh!" C-3PO exclaimed as Chewbacca guided him out of the cockpit. "Sometimes I just don't understand human behavior. After all, I'm only trying to do my job in the most —" The hatch slid shut, cutting off C-3PO's words.

Leia and Han were still inside the cockpit when the *Falcon* suddenly lurched again. Leia was thrown across the cockpit into Han, and he stumbled back into the navigator's seat. His arms encircled Leia protectively as she landed on his lap. Then, abruptly, the lurching motion stopped.

"Let go," said Leia.

"Shh!" Han said, trying to listen for any unusual sounds outside the ship as he kept his arms around Leia.

"Let go, please," Leia insisted.

"Don't get excited," Han said as he released his hold.

Leia fumed. "Captain, being held by you isn't quite enough to get me excited."

"Sorry, sweetheart," Han replied with a smirk. "We haven't got time for anything else." He opened the hatch and left the cockpit.

Leia turned to look out the window, but she was so flustered she couldn't see straight. *Why does he have to be such a jerk?* she thought. *And why do I let him get to me?* She felt almost dizzy with anger as her brain fumbled for words that she might have used to tell off Han, once and for all. Then she realized her lips were moving, mumbling words that just wouldn't come out right.

I don't know what's worse, Leia thought. *Feeling furious at Han, or feeling . . . something else.*

Something she didn't want to acknowledge.

She raised her white-gloved hand and whacked the cockpit's wall.

On Dagobah, the mist had dispersed a bit, but the swamp remained a gloomy place. Luke had retrieved a box of emergency provisions from his X-wing and set up his camp in a clearing. As he ignited a compact fusion furnace that he'd placed on a rotten log beside R2-D2, the droid beeped at him.

"What?" Luke said. "Ready for some power? Okay. Let's see now." He ran a power cable from the furnace to the droid. "Put that in there," he said to himself as he plugged the cable into R2-D2's socket. "There you go."

R2-D2 beeped, apparently content for the moment.

Luke patted R2-D2's domed head and said, "Now all I got to do is find this Yoda . . . if he even exists." To himself, he thought, *I don't even know what Yoda looks like. Since he taught Ben, he must be very old. And strong, too, if he can survive in this environ-*

ment. For the first time, Luke realized he'd been assuming Yoda was male, when in fact he didn't have any idea.

Luke sighed as he stood and looked around. "It's really a strange place to find a Jedi Master. This place gives me the creeps."

R2-D2 beeped. Even though Luke didn't have a portable droid translator, he had a feeling that the little droid agreed with him.

Luke sat down on a rock beside R2-D2 and removed a box of food rations from his stack of supplies. As he bit into a dehydrated nutrition bar, he continued, "Still . . . there's something familiar about this place."

R2-D2 beeped, wondering what Luke meant.

"I don't know . . ." Luke said, glancing at the surrounding trees. "I feel like . . ."

"Feel like what?" a strange, croaking voice interrupted.

Luke's blaster flashed from its holster and he was suddenly aiming at a short, squat alien who sat on a nearby stump. "Like we're being watched!" Luke finished.

"Away put your weapon!" the creature said as he threw his arms up over his face. "I mean you no harm." He wore a ratty old robe and clutched a small gimer stick that he held up defensively. He lowered his arms to peek over his sleeves, allowing Luke to get a better look at him. He had wrinkled green skin, long tapered ears, and large eyes that looked somehow alert and sleepy at the same time. His manner of speech was unusual and his words came out in a rhythmic croak. Luke didn't recognize the creature's species, but he appeared harmless.

The creature asked, "I am wondering, why are you here?"

"I'm looking for someone," Luke answered warily.

"Looking?" the creature said with amusement. "Found someone, you have, I would say, hmmm?" He chuckled.

Luke tried to keep from smiling as he answered, "Right."

"Help you I can. Yes, mmmm."

"I don't think so," Luke replied. Looking away as he holstered his blaster, he didn't see the creature smile slyly. Luke added, "I'm looking for a great warrior."

"Ahhh! A great warrior," the creature said, then laughed and shook his head. "Wars not make one great." Easing himself down to the ground, he held his gimer stick forward as he hobbled on his stubby tridactyl feet over to Luke's supplies. Luke had placed his nutrition bar on top of a box, and the creature picked up the bar and examined it.

"Put that down!" Luke said. "Now . . . hey!" Much to Luke's surprise, the creature had just taken a tiny bite from the bar. Luke said, "That's my dinner!"

As Luke snatched the bar and a box of rations, the creature's face twisted with disgust at the bar's taste. He said, "How you get so big, eating food of this kind?"

Luke considered finishing the nutrition bar, then thought better of it and tossed it into the swamp. "Listen, friend," he said, "we didn't mean to land in that puddle, and if we could get our ship out, we would, but we can't, so why don't you just —"

"Aww, can't you get your ship out?" the creature asked.

Luke turned to see that the creature had set aside his gimer stick and had crawled headfirst into an open container. Luke couldn't believe it. *He's rummaging through my supplies!*

"Hey, get out of there!" Luke shouted.

"Ahhh!" said the creature as he dug out an electronic device.

Luke grabbed the device and said, "Hey, you could have broken this."

Ignoring Luke, the creature dug faster, considered an item, then said, "No!" and tossed it over his shoulder. He picked out another object and tossed it after the other.

"Don't do that," Luke said. "Ohhh . . . you're making a mess."

"Oh!" cried the creature as he pulled out a tiny power lamp and regarded it with delight. He flicked it on and moved the light around his face.

"Hey, give me that!" Luke said.

"Mine!" the creature said, clutching the tiny lamp. "Or I will help you not."

"I don't want your help," Luke said. "I want my lamp back. I'm gonna need it to get out of this slimy mudhole."

The creature glared at Luke. "Mudhole? Slimy? My home this is."

While the creature faced Luke, R2-D2 opened an access panel and extended one of his manipulator arms, then clamped onto the lamp and tried to snatch it from the creature's tight grip. "Ah, ah, ah!" said the creature as he and R2-D2 began a tug-of-war contest with the lamp as the prize.

"Oh, Artoo, let him have it!" Luke said. But the droid ignored him and continued to tug.

With his free hand, the creature reached for his gimer stick and began whacking R2-D2 as he shouted, "Mine! Mine! Mine!"

"Artoo!" Luke cried out, prompting the droid to release his grip and allow the creature to win. As R2-D2 retracted his manipulator, the creature reached out with his gimer stick and playfully tapped the droid's access panel shut.

Tired of the creature, Luke said, "Now will you move along, little fella? We've got a lot of work to do."

"No! No, no!" said the creature, wielding the tiny lamp as he hobbled over to Luke. "Stay and help you, I will." The creature laughed and added, "Find your friend."

"I'm not looking for a friend," Luke said. "I'm looking for a Jedi Master."

The creature's eyes went wide and his tapered ears dipped. "Oohhh, Jedi Master. Yoda. You seek Yoda."

Now it was Luke who was surprised. Bending down so his eyes were almost level with the creature's, he said, "You know him?"

"Mmm. Take you to him, I will." The creature laughed. "Yes, yes. But now we must eat. Come. Good food. Come." The creature walked away from Luke's camp, then turned back and repeated, "Come, come."

Luke didn't trust the creature, but he wasn't afraid of him either. He turned to the astromech and said, "Artoo, stay and watch after the camp."

R2-D2 watched his master follow the creature deeper into the swamp. The droid slowly rotated his domed head clockwise, looking for any other life-forms that might be lurking in the darkness or the trees. He kept looking until he'd completed a full rotation and spotted Luke again, now farther away.

R2-D2 beeped an electronic sigh.

"Oh, where is Artoo when I need him?" C-3PO said with dismay as he shook his head. The golden droid was standing inside the *Falcon*'s main hold, and the ship was still in the cave on the moon-sized asteroid. C-3PO had just attempted to communicate with the ship's computer by whistling and beeping into a control panel on the main hold's wall. The control panel had responded with a mystifying whistle that left C-3PO slightly baffled.

Han entered the hold to check on some wires and cables. C-3PO said, "Sir, I don't know where your ship learned to communicate, but it has the most peculiar dialect. I believe, sir, it says that the power coupling on the negative axis has been polarized. I'm afraid you'll have to replace it."

Han grimaced at the droid. "Well, of *course* I'll have to replace it," he said, then walked across the hold and looked up to an open access compartment in the ceiling. Chewbacca's head peeked out to gaze down at Han, who handed a wire coil to the Wookiee and said, "Here! And Chewie . . ."

Chewbacca whined, waiting for Han to continue.

Han glanced back at C-3PO, who was still facing the control panel on the other side of the hold. Hoping only Chewbacca would hear his words, Han said in a low voice, ". . . I think we'd better replace the negative power coupling."

Chewbacca responded with an affirmative bark.

From the main hold, Han stepped through an open hatch into the adjoining circuitry bay, a narrow-walled cluster of switches and valves that also served as a shortcut — via a second hatch — to the port side cargo hold. Inside the circuitry bay, Leia had just finished welding a valve. She had removed her white gloves, and was now struggling with a lever. Her back was to Han, and she was so focused on the lever that she didn't hear his approach. But as he extended his arms past hers to reach for the lever, Leia was startled. And when she quickly realized it was Han who'd come up behind her, she was suddenly outraged. Still gripping the lever with both hands, she turned it hard with a thrust of her elbows to send Han back a step.

"Hey, Your Worship," Han said. "I'm only trying to help."

"Would you please stop calling me that?" Leia snapped, and tried turning the lever again.

Han shrugged. "Sure, Leia."

Leia broiled. She'd been putting up with Han's jibes about her royal title for so long that it seemed unfair that he should speak her name so easily. Still infuriated, she leaned into the lever and said, "Oh, you make it so difficult sometimes."

"I do, I really do," Han agreed. "You could be a little nicer, though. Come on, admit it. Sometimes you think I'm all right."

Suddenly, her hands slipped on the lever and her bare knuckles smacked against the metal. She reflexively raised one hand to her mouth, as if she might kiss away the pain, then turned to face Han and said, "Occasionally, maybe . . . when you aren't acting like a scoundrel."

"Scoundrel?" Han repeated, and took her hands in his and examined them. "Scoundrel? I like the sound of that."

Leia realized he was massaging her hands. She said, "Stop that."

"Stop what?" Han replied, trying to look innocent.

"Stop that! My hands are dirty."

"My hands are dirty, too. What are you afraid of?"

"Afraid?" The question caught Leia off guard.

Han said, "You're trembling."

"I'm not trembling," Leia countered, and realized, *He's still holding my hands.*

The space between them closed. Han said, "You like me because I'm a scoundrel. There aren't enough scoundrels in your life."

"I happen to like nice men," Leia told him. She hadn't meant to whisper, but she did.

Han replied softly, "I'm a nice man."

"No, you're not. You're . . ."

And then their lips met. For a few seconds, Leia stopped thinking about whether her hands were clean, or about the Empire, or about . . .

"Sir, sir!" C-3PO said from behind Han, and tapped him on the shoulder. "I've isolated the reverse power flux coupling."

Neither Leia nor Han had heard the droid enter the circuit bay from the main hold. Han eased out of Leia's embrace, slowly turned, and advanced toward C-3PO, blocking the droid's view of Leia and forcing him to step backward through the open hatch. Han said icily, "Thank you. Thank you very much."

Not comprehending Han's sarcasm, C-3PO said happily, "Oh, you're perfectly welcome, sir," then turned and walked away.

Han turned back to face the circuit bay's interior, but if he'd hoped to find Leia waiting for him to get rid of C-3PO, he was too late. Leia had already left through the other hatch.

CHAPTER 8

At Darth Vader's command, the fleet of Imperial Star Destroyers was escorting *Executor* through the asteroid field. The warships fired at the obstacles in their path, but the asteroids far outnumbered the combined weaponry of all the warships, and the Star Destroyers were taking a severe pummeling. Incredibly, the *Executor* remained unscathed.

A large asteroid slammed into one Star Destroyer's conning tower, and the ship was instantly engulfed by massive explosions. Evidence of the ship's loss was immediately played out on the bridge of the *Executor*, where Darth Vader stood before hologram images of the commanding officers of his escort; one hologram, an Imperial captain, quickly faded and disappeared as his transmission — along with his ship — came to a violent end.

Vader ignored the vanished hologram and faced

the three-dimensional projection of the *Avenger*'s Captain Needa, who reported, ". . . and that, Lord Vader, was the last time they appeared in any of our scopes. Considering the amount of damage we've sustained, they must have been destroyed."

"No, Captain, they're alive," Vader said. "I want every ship available to sweep the asteroid field until they are found."

With that, the conference was over. As the holograms faded out, Admiral Piett walked hurriedly onto the bridge and was almost breathless when he came to a stop before the *Executor*'s commander. Piett gasped, "Lord Vader."

One look at Piett's pallor, which was white as a sheet, and the Sith Lord knew the man was scared. "Yes, Admiral, what is it?"

Piett took a gulp of air, then tried to keep his voice from trembling as he said, "The Emperor commands you to make contact with him."

"Move the ship out of the asteroid field so that we can send a clear transmission."

"Yes, my lord," Piett said as Vader's menacing form swept off the bridge.

Vader proceeded to his personal quarters. When the *Executor* was out of the asteroid field, he stepped down from his meditation chamber to stand upon a circular black panel, a HoloNet scanner that allowed him to transmit communications across the galaxy. As the dark lord dropped to his left knee and bowed his helmeted head, the panel's outer ring was illuminated. Vader slowly raised his gaze to the empty air before him, and the emptiness was instantly filled by flickering blue light.

The light assembled to form a hologram that was nearly as tall as the room itself: a large three-dimensional image of a cloaked head with eyes that blazed wickedly from shadowy, pitted features.

There was no mistaking the face of Emperor Palpatine.

Still kneeling before the immense hologram, Vader said, "What is thy bidding, my Master?"

From light-years away, on the planet Coruscant, the Emperor said, "There is a great disturbance in the Force."

"I have felt it," Vader said.

The Emperor continued, "We have a new enemy. The young Rebel who destroyed the Death Star. I have no doubt this boy is the offspring of Anakin Skywalker."

"How is that possible?" Darth Vader managed to ask through his shock. Could it be . . . true?

"Search your feelings, Lord Vader. You will know it to be true. He could destroy us."

"He's just a boy," Vader pointed out, the belief rising within him that Anakin's son could exist. He thought, *If the Emperor knows about the boy, then he also knows the fate of Obi-Wan Kenobi.* Vader added, "Obi-Wan can no longer help him."

"The Force is strong with him," the Emperor said. "The son of Skywalker must not become a Jedi."

The Emperor had not said, in so many words, that the young Skywalker must die, which was fortunate because Vader had something else in mind. He told his master, "If he could be turned, he would become a powerful ally."

"Yes," said the Emperor, his expression thoughtful, as if he had not previously considered this possibility. Sith Lords had long maintained a rule of limiting their number to only two: one master and one apprentice — but now, the Emperor's eyes seemed to ignite, and he repeated, "Yes. He would be a great asset. Can it be done?"

"He will join us or die, Master," Vader said. He bowed, and the Emperor's hologram faded out.

Nothing will stand in my way, Darth Vader thought. *Nothing will stop me from achieving my goal. If I must search the farthest reaches of the galaxy, I will find Luke Skywalker.*

R2-D2 found Luke inside a small house made out of mud.

It was raining, and it had been easy for R2-D2 to track Luke's water-filled footprints from their camp near the spot where they'd landed on Dagobah. Although the astromech had been cautious to travel through the swampy forest on his own, he'd been even more rattled by the idea of remaining alone at the camp. Luke's footprints had led the droid to the house that had been constructed under the overhanging roots of a towering gnarltree. With its sloping outer walls, the house appeared almost organic, as if it were growing from the ground. Only the windows — smallish oval portals — and a sculpted chimney indicated the moss-covered dwelling was not a natural formation.

The structure was not much taller than the astromech himself. As the rain pelted off his domed head, R2-D2 rose up on the tips of his treads, peeked into a window, and listened. Inside, the small green-skinned creature was cooking something in a pot on a stove while Luke squatted under the low mud-packed ceiling.

"Look, I'm sure it's delicious," Luke said, eyeing the food in the pot. "I just don't understand why we can't see Yoda now."

"Patience!" the creature exclaimed. "For the Jedi it is time to eat as well. Eat, eat. Hot."

Luke moved with difficulty in the cramped quarters, but managed to sit down near the fire and serve himself from the steaming pot. He tasted the strange food and wished he hadn't.

"Good food, hm?" asked the creature. "Good, hmmm?"

But Luke wasn't interested in the food. "How far away is Yoda? Will it take us long to get there?"

"Not far," said the creature. "Yoda not far. Patience. Soon you will be with him." He tasted the food directly from the pot. "Rootleaf, I cook. Why wish you become Jedi? Hm?"

"Mostly because of my father, I guess," Luke admitted.

"Ah, father," the creature said. "Powerful Jedi was he, mmm, powerful Jedi, mmm."

"Oh, come on," Luke said, angry with the creature. "How could you know my father? You don't even know who I am. Oh, I don't know what I'm doing here. We're wasting our time."

The creature looked away from Luke and sounded disappointed as he said, "I cannot teach him. The boy has no patience."

From out of nowhere, Ben's voice answered, "He will learn patience."

Startled, Luke looked around, searching for Ben as if he might appear within the mud house.

"Hmmm," mumbled the creature. He turned

slowly, studied Luke, and said, "Much anger in him, like his father."

Ben's voice replied, "Was I any different when you taught me?"

"Hah," the creature said. "He is not ready."

Luke looked at the creature, who returned his gaze with wise old eyes. Then Luke suddenly realized the truth, and gasped, "Yoda!"

Yoda nodded.

"I *am* ready," Luke said. "I . . . Ben! I . . . I can be a Jedi. Ben, tell him I'm ready." Trying to see Ben, Luke started to get up — only to smack his head against the hut's ceiling.

"Ready, are you?" Yoda said, fixing Luke with a severe glare. "What know you of ready? For eight hundred years have I trained Jedi. My own counsel will I keep on who is to be trained! A Jedi must have the deepest commitment, the most serious mind." Yoda tilted his head slightly to address Ben, who remained invisible, as he gestured to indicate Luke. "This one a long time have I watched. All his life has he looked away . . . to the future, to the horizon. Never his mind on where he was. Hmm? What he was doing. Hmph." Yoda raised his gimer stick and jabbed Luke. "Adventure. Heh! Excitement. Heh! A Jedi craves not these things." Lowering his gimer stick, he stared at Luke. "You are reckless!"

Ben's disembodied voice said, "So was I, if you remember."

"He is too old," Yoda replied. Before the fall of the Old Republic, Jedi began their training as infants — before they could know about fear and anger — and were raised at the Jedi Temple on the planet Coruscant. One rare exception had been Luke's father, who'd been nine years of age when he'd arrived at the Jedi Temple. Yoda had been extremely reluctant to allow Luke's father to become a Jedi, and given everything that had transpired, he was even more hesitant to teach Luke. Yoda added, "Yes, too old to begin the training."

Desperate for Yoda to reconsider, Luke said, "But I've learned so much."

Yoda sighed. Addressing the invisible Ben, he asked, "Will he finish what he begins?"

Instead of allowing Ben to answer, Luke said, "I won't fail you." As Yoda's gaze returned to him, Luke felt compelled to add, "I'm not afraid."

Yoda said, "Oh," his eyes widening, and his voice dropping to a low, threatening tone, "you will be. You *will* be."

CHAPTER 9

Under the command of Captain Needa, the Imperial Star Destroyer *Avenger* cruised along the edge of the asteroid field, firing at every piece of drifting matter that strayed too close to the immense ship. Because there had been no sign that the *Millennium Falcon* had been destroyed or had left the asteroid field, Darth Vader maintained the Rebels had to be hiding on one of the larger asteroids. If they were, the *Avenger* would flush them out.

Captain Needa had dispatched Imperial TIE bombers with TIE fighter escorts, and the pilots soon arrived upon a moon-sized asteroid. There, the double-podded bombers dropped free-falling thermal detonators that exploded and left new craters on the asteroid's ravaged terrain.

Tucked away in the depths of the asteroid cave, the crew of the *Falcon* heard the distant explosions on the surface of their hiding place. While Han,

Chewbacca, and C-3PO made repairs in the main hold, Leia sat alone in the cockpit, thinking.

She wasn't thinking about how they'd get out of the cave or asteroid field, or even if they'd escape the Imperial ships. She was thinking about Han. And Luke. And how she felt about them, which was complicated. Luke was sweet and shy. He'd never told her in so many words that he was fond of her, but even before their kiss on Hoth, she knew he cared for her deeply. They had an indescribable bond.

And Han was . . . well, for all of his occasionally good qualities, he was arrogant and incredibly self-centered. Leia resented Han's behavior, the way he seemed bent on having her choose between him or Luke. *As if I don't have any more pressing concerns than Han's ego.* And Han knew Luke was fond of her, which only put more of a strain on their friendship. *Honestly, what kind of a friend is Han? I just don't know. . . .*

But he is a good kisser.

She looked at her hands. She couldn't remember when she'd put her white gloves back on, but she was wearing them now. It wasn't that cold in the *Falcon,* but gloves were good for other things, like discouraging bare-handed massages. *Why invite trouble?* Still, she'd been surprised by the warmth and gentleness of Han's touch. . . .

This is madness! What am I, a schoolgirl? There's

116

a war on and I have a job to do. I don't have the time or energy for this! I should just tell Han to —

She saw something move outside the cockpit window. She thought, *Maybe my eyes are getting tired?* Leaning forward in her seat, she peered into the darkness.

Suddenly, a leathery, flying creature appeared and suctioned its face against the window with a loud slap. Startled, Leia screamed and fell back against her seat, then turned and hurried out of the cockpit.

In the main hold, C-3PO was trying yet again to engage Han's attention. "Sir, if I may venture an opinion —"

"I'm not really interested in your opinion, Three-pio," Han interrupted.

Leia ran into the hold, past the droid, and found Han and Chewbacca facing a wall, making repairs to exposed cables. She said, "There's something out there."

Chewbacca and Han, both wearing welding goggles, looked almost comical as they turned to face Leia. Han raised his goggles and asked, "Where?"

"Outside, in the cave."

As if in response, there came a sharp banging on the hull.

C-3PO cried, "There it is! Listen! Listen!"

The noise came again. Chewbacca barked anxiously.

"I'm going out there," Han said. He stepped over to a wall-mounted rack of supplies.

Leia said, "Are you crazy?"

"I just got this bucket back together," Han said. "I'm not going to let something tear it apart." He reached to a nearby supply rack and grabbed a breath mask, a portable life-support unit that would allow him to breathe in the cave.

Leia said, "Oh, then I'm going with you." She took a breath mask and hurried after Han, then Chewbacca did the same.

C-3PO stood nervously in the hold. To the departing figures, he said, "I think it might be better if I stay behind and guard the ship." Another mysterious noise echoed off the hull, causing the droid to tremble and mutter, "Oh, no."

At the top of the ship's landing ramp, Han, Leia, and Chewbacca placed their breath masks over their noses and mouths. The landing ramp extended to the cave floor, and Han walked down it, followed by Leia and Chewbacca. Han had his blaster pistol out and Chewbacca carried his Wookiee bowcaster. Leia held her empty hands out at her sides and thought, *Shouldn't I be carrying a glow rod or something?*

There was a heavy mist in the cave, which was illuminated only by the *Falcon*'s landing lights. Han stepped cautiously onto the cave floor. While his eyes searched for anything unusual on his ship's shadowy exterior, Leia followed. Testing her footing, she said, "This ground sure feels strange. It doesn't feel like rock."

Han looked at the swirling mist and said, "There's an awful lot of moisture in here."

"I don't know," Leia remarked vaguely, then added, "I have a bad feeling about this."

"Yeah," Han agreed.

Suddenly, Chewbacca barked through his face mask and pointed toward the *Falcon*'s cockpit. Han moved fast, firing his blaster at the indicated spot. There was a loud screech, then Han yelled to Leia, "Watch out!"

A leathery creature tumbled from the cockpit to the ground. Han stepped over and bent down to examine the dead beast, saying, "It's all right. It's all right."

Chewbacca walked over to Han and whimpered.

Han said, "Yeah, what I thought. Mynock." Han and Chewbacca had encountered mynocks before: silicon-based parasites that feed on energy from starships. Han said, "Chewie, check the rest of the ship, make sure there are no more attached. They're chewing on the power cables."

"Mynocks?" Leia asked. *I've never heard of them.*

"Go on inside," Han said. "We'll clean them off if there are any more."

But before Leia could return to the landing ramp, a swarm of mynocks swooped past her. She raised her arms in front of her head to protect herself, then more mynocks flew at Chewbacca, who swung his bowcaster at them.

Inside the *Falcon*, C-3PO entered the cockpit to see what was going on outside. The droid nearly jumped out of his metal plating when several mynocks flapped their wings against the cockpit window. "Ohhh!" C-3PO shouted. "Go away! Go away!" He waved his arms at them. "Beastly thing. Shoo! Shoo!"

Chewbacca fired at one, and the fired bolt of energy slammed into the cave wall — causing the entire cave to rumble.

Han stood still, listening to the sounds in the cave. The mynocks had suddenly flown away, but why? Han thought about it, then said, "Wait a minute . . ." He aimed his blaster at the cave floor and fired.

More rumbling, only worse. The entire cave suddenly tilted hard to the side, nearly launching Han, Leia, and Chewbacca off their feet. As the cave rocked around them, they rushed across the misty floor and up the landing ramp.

Running for the main hold, Han tore off his breath mask and shouted, "Pull her up, Chewie. Let's get out of here!"

Chewbacca ran to the cockpit. Leia followed Han

into the hold, where they nearly fell into C-3PO. As Han checked the scopes on a control panel, Leia said, "The Empire is still out there. I don't think it's wise to —"

"No time to discuss this in committee," Han interrupted.

"I am not a committee!" Leia protested as Han bolted for the cockpit. The *Millennium Falcon*'s main engines began to whine. Leia went after Han, stumbling into the corridor walls as another quake rocked the ship.

When Leia and Han entered the cockpit, Chewbacca was already hanging on to his seat. As Han jumped behind his controls and pulled back on the throttle, Leia insisted, "You can't make the jump to lightspeed in this asteroid field!"

"Sit down, sweetheart," Han replied. "We're taking off!"

The cave quake diminished as the ship moved forward. C-3PO stepped into the cockpit just as Chewbacca noticed something ahead. The Wookiee barked.

C-3PO pointed to the cockpit window and exclaimed, "Look!"

Han said, "I see it, I see it."

They were fast approaching a row of jagged white stalagmites and stalactites that surrounded the cave's entrance. But as the ship hurtled forward, the jagged formations appeared to be closing in on each other, and the entrance grew smaller.

Han pulled hard on the throttle to increase speed.

"We're doomed!" the droid cried.

"The cave is collapsing!" Leia shouted.

"This is no cave," Han said.

Leia gasped, "What?" Then she realized Han was right. They weren't looking at the mouth of the cave, but the mouth of an enormous monster. The jagged rock formations were really teeth.

Chewbacca howled as the *Millennium Falcon* zoomed forward and rolled on its side to pass — just barely — between two of the gigantic white teeth. The jaws quickly slammed closed behind them. The ship ascended, and the monster — a space slug — raised its head after them and tried for another bite but missed. The *Falcon* was too fast. As the ship sped away from the asteroid, the space slug tilted its massive head, then withdrew and slid back into its cave.

The *Falcon* headed once more into the asteroid belt.

CHAPTER 10

Yoda was riding in a pack strapped to Luke's back. Already sweating in his sleeveless tunic, Luke grabbed hold of a thick vine that stretched down from a high tree to the Dagobah swamp. He pulled himself up, hand over hand, carrying Yoda with him. Winged creatures flew through the humid air, but Luke ignored them.

At a designated branch, Luke turned, grabbed another vine, and swung away from the tree, down to the ground. He landed on solid soil, flipped his body forward over a broad root, and began to run through the swamp. As Luke raced in and out of the heavy ground fog, Yoda spoke to the back of Luke's head, urging him on.

"Run!" Yoda said as he clung to Luke's shoulders. "Yes. A Jedi's strength flows from the Force. But beware of the dark side. Anger . . . fear . . . aggression. The dark side of the Force are they. Easily they flow, quick to join you in a fight. If once you start down the dark path, forever will it dominate your destiny, consume you it will, as it did Obi-Wan's apprentice."

Luke came to an abrupt stop and said, "Vader." Breathing hard, he turned his head slightly to address Yoda and asked, "Is the dark side stronger?"

Yoda answered, "No . . . no . . . no. Quicker, easier, more seductive."

"But how am I to know the good side from the bad?"

"You will know," Yoda assured his new pupil, his voice a soothing rasp in Luke's ear. "When you are calm, at peace. Passive. A Jedi uses the Force for knowledge and defense, never for attack."

"But tell me why I can't —"

"No, no, there is no why," Yoda interrupted. "Nothing more will I teach you today. Clear your mind of questions. Mmm. Mmmmmmm."

Luke closed his eyes to meditate.

R2-D2 beeped in the distance as Luke lowered Yoda to the ground. While the aged Jedi settled himself on a wide root, Luke stepped over to a tree branch, where he'd placed his shirt and weapon belt.

As Luke pulled on his shirt, he sensed something strange and deadly in the air. He turned to see a huge, dead, black tree, its trunk surrounded by a

Luke Skywalker on his tauntaun, looking for life readings on the ice-planet Hoth.

Will Luke free himself before the wampa returns?

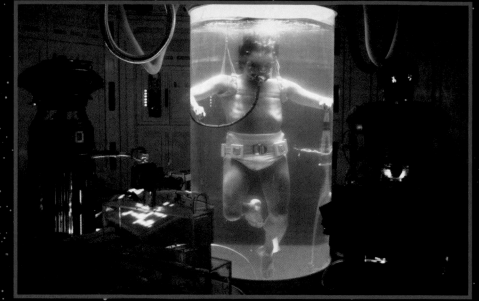

Luke recuperates in a bacta tank while . . .

. . . Chewbacca helps stage an ambush.

**Imperial probe droid found
—and destroyed!**

Deadly AT-AT walkers attack the Rebels.
The Battle of Hoth begins!

The Rebel Alliance deploys its troops.

Darth Vader searches for his enemies . . .

. . . who have just blasted off in the
Millennium Falcon.

"You're not actually going into an asteroid field?"
asks Princess Leia Organa.

The *Millennium Falcon* searches for a hiding place away from
enemy fire.

Luke and R2-D2 land on the strange,
swamp-like planet of Dagobah . . .

. . . where a small creature surprises them.

Armed with his lightsaber, Luke
learns to confront the dark side.

"There's something out there!" says Leia from inside the *Millennium Falcon*.

A last-minute escape!

"A Jedi's strength flows from the Force," says Yoda.

Han and Leia are greeted by Lando Calrissian
as they arrive at Cloud City.

"How you doing, you old pirate?"
Lando asks Han.

Chewbacca has found C-3PO, or what's left of him.

"I love you," says Leia to Han.

Carbon freezing: a cruel punishment for Han Solo.

"Obi-Wan has taught you well," says Darth Vader.

Chewie and Leia lose patience with Lando.

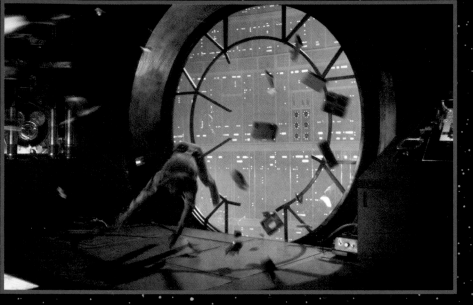

A broken window means Luke must get a grip . . . . fast.

Inside an enormous reactor shaft,

The *Millennium Falcon* escapes the grasp of an
Imperial Star Destroyer.

C-3PO, R2-D2, Luke, and Leia ponder an
uncertain future.

few feet of water. Giant, twisted roots formed a dark and sinister-looking cave on one side. Luke stared at the tree and a chill ran down his spine.

"There's something not right here," he said. "I feel cold, death."

"That place . . ." Yoda said from his seat, "is strong with the dark side of the Force. A domain of evil it is. In you must go."

Luke thought, *He actually wants me to go in?* But he also somehow knew the journey was necessary. It seemed the place was silently calling to him, beckoning. Hesitant, Luke asked, "What's in there?"

Yoda said, "Only what you take with you."

Luke looked warily between the tree and Yoda, then started to strap on his weapon belt.

Seeing this, Yoda said, "Your weapons . . . you will not need them."

Luke gave the tree a long look, then shook his head and strapped on his belt. Yoda shrugged. As Luke walked away, the little droid trembled.

Luke brushed aside some hanging vines, then lowered himself into a hole. In the darkness, he could barely make out the passage that lay before him, but he proceeded deeper into it. There were roots, tangled and twisting up the walls, and the smell of rot and decay was everywhere. Could these roots bring life to the tree above? Somehow it seemed doubtful.

The space widened around him, and then he saw

something move in front of him. There was a shadowy form, then mechanical breathing sounds, and a sense of dread.

Darth Vader.

The dark lord appeared from the blackness, and Luke took a few steps back. Time seemed to slow down, but Luke's mind raced: *How did Vader get to Dagobah? Is he looking for Master Yoda? Or is he here for . . . me?* Then he remembered his lightsaber, and in an instant, the cave was illuminated by its blue blade.

Vader drew and activated his own red lightsaber, crossing his blade with Luke's. Luke tried to concentrate but felt himself being distracted, drawn into the sound of labored breathing that came from Vader's helmet. Then Vader attacked.

But Luke was ready. He angled his blade defensively to block Vader's blade, and there was a loud, electric clash between the two lightsabers. The dark lord pulled back and swung again; Luke parried and prepared for Vader's next assault. Their lightsabers again connected with a loud crackle of energy, until Luke broke free, swung hard —

— and cut off Vader's head.

Sparks showered up from the neck of Vader's decapitated form, his body toppled, and his helmet rolled across the cave floor.

Luke stared at the helmet, and its black oval lenses

seemed to stare back. Then there was another shower of sparks, and the helmet's faceplate burned away. The smoke cleared to reveal a face, cradled in the smoldering, broken shell of Vader's helmet.

The face was Luke's own.

This isn't really happening, Luke thought as he stared at the head, into its cold, dead eyes. *It's all some kind of a hallucination or nightmare. But . . . what could it possibly mean?*

While Luke made his way out of the cave, Yoda remained seated on the root. He looked at the ground and shook his head. Although Luke did not yet comprehend what had happened in the cave, Yoda knew that it had been a test. And that Luke had failed.

CHAPTER 11

On the bridge of the *Executor*, Darth Vader approached an assembly of six bizarre figures. Each had Vader's clearance to be on the *Executor*, but none were entirely welcome.

"Bounty hunters," Admiral Piett muttered to two Imperial controllers on the bridge's lower level. "We don't need that scum."

"Yes, sir," agreed one controller.

"Those Rebels won't escape us," Piett added as he turned away from the controllers. He was immediately distracted by a growl from above. He looked up to see one of the bounty hunters, a tall humanoid reptilian whose long, clawed arms stuck out from an ill-fitting flight suit, which Piett guessed had once belonged to a human pilot. The hunter stared down from the upper level and bared his fangs at Piett.

Piett stared back, hesitant to make a move that the creature might interpret as sudden. But the staring contest came to an end when another controller approached Piett and said, "Sir, we have a priority signal from the Star Destroyer *Avenger*."

"Right," Piett answered as he tore his gaze from the hunter and followed the controller to a console.

The menacing reptilian's name was Bossk, and he remained standing at the edge of the bridge's upper level while Darth Vader surveyed the other bounty hunters. There was Dengar, a brutal-looking man with a bandaged head who wore Imperial surplus armor; IG-88, an assassin droid that resembled nothing more than an ambulatory arsenal; Zuckuss, an insectlike alien whose face was partially concealed by a breathing mask, and his partner 4-Lom, a late-model protocol droid.

Finally, there was the hunter who was widely regarded as the most dangerous of all: Boba Fett.

Fett was clad in old green battle armor that he wore over a pale gray reinforced double-layer flight suit. His head was completely concealed by a green helmet with a T-shaped macrobinocular viewplate and a retractable targeting rangefinder that allowed him to view his surroundings without turning his head. He carried numerous concealed weapons, and openly clutched a late-model modified EE-3 blaster rifle. On his back, he wore a missile-firing jetpack.

All the bounty hunters listened as Darth Vader said,

"There will be a substantial reward for the one who finds the *Millennium Falcon*. You are free to use any methods necessary, but I want them alive." Vader extended a black-gloved finger at Boba Fett and stressed, "No disintegrations."

"As you wish," Fett said, his voice a nasty rasp. He was already on retainer for Jabba the Hutt, the Tatooine-based gangster who'd placed a bounty on Han Solo. Jabba also wanted the *Falcon*'s captain alive, so Fett had no intention of killing him. If he did the job right, he would be rewarded by the Empire *and* the Hutt.

Boba Fett had another reason for wanting to capture Solo. Until recently, he'd had a perfect record for getting the job done. Any job, no matter how dirty or tough. But several weeks earlier, Fett had made a mistake: Another assignment had left him temporarily unable to follow a tip on Solo's whereabouts, so he'd subcontracted Dengar, Bossk, and another bounty hunter named Skorr to search for Solo. The hunters not only found and captured Solo, but delivered him to the planet Ord Mantell, where Fett had arranged to meet them. But shortly after Boba Fett arrived on Ord Mantell, Skorr was dead — and Han Solo was gone.

Both Dengar and Bossk had failed enough bounty hunts to assure that neither would ever have a perfect record, but Boba Fett was different. He had his reputation to maintain.

Darth Vader turned as an excited Admiral Piett ascended to the upper level. "Lord Vader!" Piett said. "My lord, we have them."

The *Avenger* had the *Millennium Falcon* on the run. The destroyer fired lasers at the smaller ship, which weaved to evade not only the blasts from behind but the few asteroids that remained in its path.

Inside the *Falcon*'s cockpit, Leia and C-3PO sat in the rear seats and watched nervously as Han and Chewbacca prepared for the jump to hyperspace. Glancing out the cockpit window, the droid said, "Oh, thank goodness we're coming out of the asteroid field."

"Let's get out of here," Han said. "Ready for lightspeed?" He reached for the throttle. "One . . . two . . . three!"

On "three," Han pulled back on the throttle. Outside the cockpit, the view of distant stars remained unchanged. Again.

"It's not fair!" Han protested.

Leia rolled her eyes and gaped. Chewbacca whimpered and raised his furry hands in defeat.

"The transfer circuits are all working," Han said, then insisted, "It's not my fault!"

Leia couldn't believe it. "No lightspeed?"

"It's not my fault," Han said again.

Suddenly, the *Falcon* was slammed hard as Imperial laserfire struck the stern.

C-3PO glanced at a sensor scope and said, "Sir, we just lost the main rear deflector shield. One more direct hit on the back quarter and we're done for."

Han looked to Chewbacca and said, "Turn her around."

Chewbacca barked in puzzlement.

"I said turn her around!" Han said, jumping out of his seat to throw a set of switches on the cockpit wall. "I'm going to put all power in the front shield."

"You're going to attack them?!" Leia said with alarm as Han jumped back behind the controls.

When Han didn't reply, C-3PO informed him, "Sir, the odds of surviving a direct assault on an Imperial Star Destroyer —"

"Shut up!" Leia shouted.

Han banked hard to port, then made a steep, twisting turn. In the next moment, the *Falcon* was racing toward the infinitely more powerful Destroyer.

Standing on the *Avenger*'s bridge, watching the *Falcon* through the viewport, Captain Needa couldn't believe his eyes. "They're moving to attack position!" he exclaimed. "Shields up!"

The Star Destroyer's laser cannons fired at the oncoming ship, but none hit their target. From Needa's position, it looked like the *Falcon* was coming straight for the bridge.

Out of pure human reflex, Needa and his men ducked as the Rebel ship roared past the viewport. But instead of the expected collision, there was suddenly silence. Needa looked out the viewport.

The *Falcon* was nowhere to be seen.

Needa turned to the tracking officer and ordered, "Track them. They may come around for another pass."

The tracking officer checked his console screen, then said, "Captain Needa, the ship no longer appears on our scopes."

"They can't have disappeared," Needa said. "No ship that small has a cloaking device."

Consulting his screen again, the tracking officer said, "Well, there's no trace of them, sir."

The *Avenger*'s communications officer looked up from his console. "Captain, Lord Vader demands an update on the pursuit."

Needa drew a breath, then turned to his first officer and said, "Get a shuttle ready. I shall assume full responsibility for losing them and apologize to Lord Vader. Meanwhile, continue to scan the area."

"Yes, Captain Needa," said the officer.

As Captain Needa left the bridge and headed for

the shuttle hangar, the *Avenger* changed course to rendezvous with the Imperial fleet.

On Dagobah, Luke's muscles strained as his palms pressed against the dry mud. He was standing on his hands, with his legs extended up into the air and Yoda perched on his right foot. Then Luke slowly lifted his right hand and felt his weight shift down the length of his left arm.

Still balanced on Luke's foot, Yoda instructed, "Use the Force, yes. Now . . . the stone."

A short distance from Luke, two rocks rested in the dirt. Luke stared at them and concentrated. One of the rocks lifted from the ground.

"Feel it," Yoda intoned.

And even though Luke wasn't touching the rock, he could sense its texture and weight. *It's dry on the top, slick on the bottom . . . not heavy at all.* The rock hovered, then came to a gentle rest on the other.

R2-D2 was standing at the water's edge, watching Luke and Yoda with fascination, when he heard a bubbling noise from behind. The astromech rotated his domed head and saw the source of the sound: Luke's X-wing was rapidly sinking into the mucky water.

The little droid beeped frantically, distracting Luke.

"Concentrate!" Yoda scolded, but it was too late. The upper rock slid off the lower, and Luke collapsed, sending Yoda tumbling across the ground.

Luke rose quickly and hurried over to R2-D2, who was now chirping wildly. Luke watched his ship sink under the water until only the upper starboard wing remained visible above the surface.

"Oh, no," Luke said. "We'll never get it out now."

"So certain are you," Yoda replied. He had righted himself from the fall to sit facing Luke, and he wore an expression of mild contempt. "Always with you it cannot be done. Hear you nothing that I say?"

"Master, moving stones around is one thing," Luke said, then gestured to the X-wing. "This is totally different."

"No!" Yoda said. "No different! Only different in your mind. You must unlearn what you have learned."

"All right," Luke said. "I'll give it a try."

"No!" Yoda protested fiercely. "Try not. *Do*. Or do not. There is no try."

Luke turned his body to face the water. He closed his eyes as he extended his right hand, aiming his outstretched fingers at the submerged X-wing. He concentrated.

He sensed the X-wing's dimensions and sharp contours, felt the weight of the ship and the water's pressure against its hull. Was the starfighter underwater so different from a small rock on dry land? Eyes still closed, Luke felt a stirring from within, and knew the X-wing was rising.

As the starfighter's nose lifted from the muck, Yoda's eyes went wide with anticipation. But then Luke grimaced . . . *It's too big . . . too heavy . . .* and the X-wing sank again.

Looking defeated and drained, Luke turned away from the shore and dropped to the ground beside Yoda. He told the Jedi Master, "I can't." Then he added, "It's too big."

"Size matters not," Yoda said. "Look at me. Judge me by my size, do you? Mm?"

Luke shook his head.

"Mmmm," Yoda murmured. "And well you should not. For my ally is the Force. And a powerful ally it is. Life creates it, makes it grow. Its energy surrounds us and binds us. Luminous beings are we . . ." He pinched Luke's shoulder. ". . . not this crude matter."

Yoda made a sweeping gesture and continued, "You must feel the Force around you. Here, between you . . . me . . . the tree . . . the rock . . . everywhere! Yes, even between the land and the ship!"

Thoroughly discouraged, Luke said, "You want the impossible." He got up and started to walk away.

Yoda sighed. Slowly, he bowed his head and closed his eyes. Then he raised his small right hand in the direction of the sunken X-wing.

The starfighter began to rise again.

R2-D2 watched the displaced water flow off the

starfighter as it lifted from the swamp. Long strands of moss and weeds dangled from the ship as it rose higher. The little droid began beeping wildly.

Luke heard R2-D2's cries and turned back. The X-wing was hovering high over the water's surface. He looked to Yoda, then back to the X-wing. The ship slowly traveled through the air, then descended to land on an area of moss-covered ground.

Luke examined the starfighter, brushing some muck from its hull to convince himself this wasn't another hallucination. The X-wing was real, all right. Luke turned back to Yoda. He knelt before the Jedi Master and gasped, "I don't . . . I don't believe it."

With a touch of sadness in his voice, Yoda said, "That is why you fail."

CHAPTER 12

After the *Avenger* met up with the Imperial fleet, Captain Needa traveled by shuttle to board the *Executor*. Minutes later, on the *Executor*'s bridge, Captain Needa spoke the words that would be his last. As Vader choked him from afar, he clutched desperately at his throat. But it was no use. He dropped to his knees, lifted his head, and tried to rise, then collapsed at the feet of Darth Vader.

Vader said, "Apology accepted, Captain Needa."

As two black-uniformed Imperial soldiers lifted Needa's lifeless body and carried it from the bridge, the Sith Lord walked to the nearby command console, where Admiral Piett and his aides were examining data. Seeing Vader approach, Piett stepped away from his console and stood at attention.

"Lord Vader," Piett said, "our ships have completed their scan of the area and found nothing. If the *Millennium Falcon* went into lightspeed, it'll be on the other side of the galaxy by now."

"Alert all commands," Vader said. "Calculate every possible destination along their last known trajectory."

"Yes, my lord," Piett said. "We'll find them."

Vader loomed over Piett and warned, "Don't fail me again, Admiral."

Piett swallowed hard, then turned to an aide and ordered, "Alert all commands. Deploy the fleet."

The *Millennium Falcon*'s possible destination routes were quickly computed by the Imperials. As the *Executor* and Star Destroyers prepared to leave the area, every Imperial helmsman, navigator, controller, and technician kept their keen eyes on their consoles and monitors. And because all sensors had already indicated the *Falcon* had vanished from the sector, not one Imperial soldier thought to look out a window.

But even if anyone had looked directly at the port aft of *Avenger*'s command tower, they might not have immediately spotted the *Millennium Falcon*, which rested flat against the destroyer's hull, right where Han Solo had landed it. Because of the *Falcon*'s faded white exterior, the Corellian transport blended right in with the Imperial ship.

"Captain Solo, this time you have gone too far," C-3PO said from his seat behind Chewbacca in the cockpit.

Chewbacca growled at the golden droid. C-3PO answered, "No, I will not be quiet, Chewbacca. Why doesn't anyone listen to me?"

Leia leaned forward in her seat behind Han. Both were looking out the cockpit window, watching the Star Destroyers move off in different directions.

"The fleet is beginning to break up," Han said. He glanced at Chewbacca and said, "Go back and stand by the manual release for the landing claw."

"I really don't see how that is going to help," the droid said as Chewbacca climbed from his seat and moved out of the cockpit. "Surrender is a perfectly acceptable alternative in extreme circumstances. The Empire may be gracious enough —"

C-3PO's sentence was cut short by Leia, who'd reached behind the droid's neck to switch him off. The droid slumped forward against his seat belt and remained silent.

"Thank you," Han said.

Leia felt the need to ask, "What did you have in mind for your next move?"

Gesturing at the Star Destroyers, Han replied, "Well, if they follow standard Imperial procedure, they'll dump their garbage before they go to lightspeed, and then we just float away."

"With the rest of the garbage," Leia said, which made Han wince. "Then what?"

"Then we've got to find a safe port somewhere

around here." Han activated a mapscreen on his control panel, and Leia leaned closer to him to study the map. Han asked, "Got any ideas?"

"No. Where are we?"

"The Anoat system."

"Anoat system," Leia repeated thoughtfully. "There's not much there."

"No," Han said, then noticed something on the map. "Well, wait. This is interesting. Lando."

"Lando system?"

Han grinned and said, "Lando's not a system, he's a man. Lando Calrissian. He's a card player, gambler — scoundrel." He glanced at Leia and added, "You'd like him."

Leia smirked. "Thanks."

Han returned his attention to the mapscreen. "Bespin," he said, giving the destination more consideration. "It's pretty far, but I think we can make it."

Reading the displayed data on Bespin, Leia said, "A mining colony?"

"Yeah," Han said. "A Tibanna gas mine. Lando conned somebody out of it." He leaned back in his seat and added, "We go back a long way, Lando and me."

From Han's tone, Leia got the impression that his history with Lando wasn't entirely friendly. "Can you trust him?" she asked.

"No," Han admitted. "But he has got no love for the Empire, I can tell you that."

Chewbacca barked over the ship's intercom and Han quickly changed his readouts. Then he stretched to look out the cockpit window and saw a wide, rectangular hatch open on the Star Destroyer's hull. Speaking into the intercom, Han said, "Here we go, Chewie. Stand by." He waited for several large bits of metal refuse to float out of the open hatch, then said, "Detach!"

The *Falcon*'s landing claw released, and the transport drifted away along with the debris that trailed from the Imperial cruiser. As they drifted farther from the ship, Leia felt increasingly elated. Granted, she would have been more relieved if the *Falcon*'s hyperdrive had actually kicked in when it was supposed to, but if it hadn't been for Han's quick thinking and cunning piloting skills . . . *I have to give him some credit.*

As Han kept his eyes on the departing Star Destroyer, Leia touched his shoulder and said, "You do have your moments. Not many of them, but you do have them." She kissed his cheek, then settled back into her seat.

The destroyer's three main ion engines flared brightly, then the ship launched forward and vanished into the distance. Han fired the *Falcon*'s sublight engines and veered away from the debris, heading in the opposite direction of the Imperial ship's trajectory.

As the *Falcon* sped away from the debris trail, there was a sudden flare from behind a large piece of drifting scrap — which wasn't scrap at all. It was *Slave I*, a highly modified *Firespray*-class patrol-and-attack ship, equipped with numerous hidden weapons. And it was the personal transport for the bounty hunter Boba Fett.

Fett had correctly calculated that the *Millennium Falcon* had never actually escaped from the *Avenger*, and had only avoided detection. Now, as he accelerated after Han Solo's ship, it seemed his calculations would pay off.

Slave I had long-range sensor scopes and an illegal masking-and-jamming system that made it virtually invisible on most scanners. The special technology had allowed Boba Fett to infiltrate the Imperial Fleet, locate the *Millennium Falcon*, and maneuver *Slave I* into the *Avenger*'s debris trail without alerting anyone to his presence. Fett was so confident in *Slave I*'s supreme stealth that he kept the escaping *Falcon* within visual range as he computed its trajectory.

Fett checked his computer readout: The Rebel ship was heading for the Bespin system. As the *Falcon* was traveling at sublight speed, the bounty hunter concluded there was something wrong with the ship's hyperdrive. And because *Slave I*'s hyperdrive was fully operational, Fett knew he'd be able to reach Bespin before Solo.

The bounty hunter considered his next move, then transmitted a coded message to the *Executor*.

On Dagobah, R2-D2 stood near some equipment cases and watched as Yoda continued to instruct Luke. The Jedi trainee was yet again standing on his hands with his feet extended up, but R2-D2 noticed Yoda had refrained from perching on one of Luke's feet this time, opting instead to remain on the ground.

Yoda said, "Concentrate."

Luke closed his eyes. Two equipment cases rose from the ground, then hung suspended in the air.

"Feel the Force flow," Yoda said, his voice soothing. "Yes."

The astromech droid felt himself being lifted, and momentarily thought he might have unwittingly stepped on the back of a rising creature. When he realized the only thing between him and the ground was Luke's will, the little droid beeped nervously.

"Good," Yoda said. "Calm, yes. Through the Force, things you will see."

Still standing on his hands, Luke opened his eyes, then closed them again.

"Other places," Yoda continued. "The future . . . the past. Old friends long gone."

Suddenly, Luke's mind was overwhelmed by an unexpected vision. His eyes opened wide and he shouted, "Han! Leia!"

The suspended objects fell to the ground. Unlike the equipment cases, R2-D2 screeched on the way down. Luke tumbled and rolled over onto his side.

Yoda shook his head. "Hmm. Control, control. You must learn control."

Luke looked dazed and rattled. He wanted to tell Yoda about the vision, but wasn't sure how to put it into words. Hesitantly, he said, "I saw . . . I saw a city in the clouds."

"Mmm," Yoda muttered. "Friends you have there."

Luke looked anguished as he recalled, "They were in pain."

Yoda nodded. "It is the future you see."

"Future?" Luke said with alarm. "Will they die?"

Yoda closed his eyes, meditated briefly, then opened his eyes and gazed at Luke. "Difficult to see. Always in motion is the future."

Luke thought, *If I saw the future, is it also possible for me to change it?* He pushed himself up from the ground and said, "I've got to go to them."

Yoda sighed. "Decide you must how to serve them best. If you leave now, help them you could. But you would destroy all for which they have fought and suffered."

Luke couldn't stand the thought of his friends suffering. He thought, *Could Yoda be right? If I try to help, would I really be doing the wrong thing?* He gazed hard at Yoda, hoping the Jedi Master would suggest other alternatives for action, or interpret brighter possibilities for the future.

Yoda remained silent. And in the silence, Luke knew there was nothing left to say, because Yoda was right: The future was difficult to see.

Luke nodded sadly.

And Yoda knew Luke had already decided what to do.

CHAPTER 13

The Cloud City Control Wing Guard pilot was getting on Han Solo's nerves.

"No, I don't have a landing permit," Han snarled into the *Millennium Falcon*'s cockpit comlink.

Behind Han, Leia leaned forward and looked left, past Chewbacca and out the cockpit window, to see the two twin-pod cloud cars that had appeared from out of nowhere. The cloud cars were so close that Leia could distinguish the Wing Guard pilot whose mouth moved in synchronization with the voice from the comlink.

Leia thought, *Welcome to Bespin.*

Bespin was a giant, gaseous planet, a world of billowing clouds and endless sky. Its atmosphere was a prime source of valuable Tibanna gas, which was used as either a conducting agent to boost blaster firepower or a hyperdrive coolant. The world was also home to Cloud City, the largest of the airborne Tibanna factories, and the *Falcon*'s destination.

The *Falcon* had descended through Bespin's upper altitudes until it entered a narrow band of breathable air. Not only breathable, but breathtaking for its sweeping views of cloud formations. The initial sight of Bespin had seemed warm and inviting, especially to those who'd so recently endured the frigid climate of Hoth. But when the two twin-pod cloud cars had suddenly swooped into view, it had become quickly evident that the Bespin skies were far from entirely friendly.

Han said into the comlink, "I'm trying to reach Lando Calrissian." He'd barely uttered Lando's name when the nearest cloud car fired a blaster cannon and flak exploded outside the *Falcon*. "Whoa!" Han shouted. "Wait a minute! Let me explain."

From the *Falcon*'s intercom, the Cloud City Wing Guard pilot said, "You will not deviate from your present course."

"Rather touchy, aren't they?" a reactivated C-3PO commented from the seat behind Chewbacca.

To Han, Leia said, "I thought you knew this person."

Chewie barked and growled at Han. Han replied, "Well, that was a long time ago. I'm sure he's forgotten about that."

From the intercom, the Cloud City Wing Guard

said, "Permission granted to land on Platform three-two-seven."

Han wanted to say something else into the comlink, but instead he said, "Thank you," and switched off.

Chewbacca looked at Han and grunted. Han glanced back at Leia and C-3PO and said, "There's nothing to worry about. We go way back, Lando and me."

"Who's worried?" said Leia, clinging to her seat.

The two cloud cars escorted the *Falcon* across the sky, and it wasn't long before Cloud City came into view. Sixteen kilometers in diameter and seventeen kilometers tall, the 392-level floating city resembled an immense wheel lying on its side. The entire city was held aloft by 3,600 repulsorlift engines, and had a long central stalk that dropped down beneath it and ended in a unipod. The unipod used tractor beams to draw Tibanna gas up into the city's gas refineries.

As the *Falcon* neared the city, Leia could see it was slowly rotating, and that the cityscape had a rounded, decorative design with tall towers and wide plazas. The long shadows of streamlined skyscrapers swept over the *Falcon*'s exterior as it passed over the city. The two cloud cars stuck with the Corellian transport.

Platform 327 was a circular platform at the end of

an extended walkway that was connected to an upper level of a skyscraper. The *Falcon*'s landing jets fired, and the ship touched down neatly. The cloud car escorts flew off.

Steam vented from the jet exhausts as the ship's landing ramp lowered. Han stepped down to the platform, followed by Chewbacca, Leia, and a very hesitant C-3PO. They looked to the far end of the platform, where a rectangular door was visible against the high wall of the skyscraper. The door was closed.

"Oh," C-3PO said. "No one to meet us."

They remained at the bottom of the landing ramp, watching the distant door and waiting. A warm wind moaned softly across the city.

Leia said, "I don't like this."

"Well, what would you like?" Han snapped, as if they had any options.

Hoping to sound optimistic, C-3PO stated, "Well, they *did* let us land."

"Look, don't worry," Han said, turning to Leia. "Everything's going to be fine. Trust me."

At the end of the platform, the rectangular door slid up to reveal two men engaged in a discussion. Because of the distance and the light from inside the open doorway, the two appeared as silhouettes, but Han's keen eyes recognized one of them.

"See?" Han said to Leia, gesturing to the doorway. "My friend."

The two men exited the door and were followed by six uniformed guards. Together, they headed up the walkway toward the *Falcon*.

Han stepped over to Chewbacca and muttered, "Keep your eyes open, huh?"

Chewbacca let out a growl as Han headed down the walkway.

As the figures approached, Leia was able to make out the two who walked in front of the six guards. The taller one was a dashing brown-skinned man with wavy black hair and a thin mustache; a silk-lined blue cape was draped across his shoulders and, from the way he moved, he looked like the man in charge. The other man was bald with pale white skin, and was primarily distinguished by the computer bracket that was wrapped around the back of his hairless head.

Han smiled at the approaching couple and said, "Hey?"

The caped man stopped two meters shy of Han. He fixed Han with an angry glare, then shook his head and said, "Why, you slimy, double-crossing, no-good swindler! You've got a lot of guts coming here after what you pulled."

Han pointed to himself innocently, and silently mouthed, *Me?*

The caped man walked slowly toward Han until the two men were face-to-face. Then, without warning, he moved fast and threw a jab at Han. Han blocked with his arm, but the jab was a fake, and the man threw his arms around Han and embraced him. Clearly, whatever gripe Lando Calrissian had with Han was a thing of the past.

Lando laughed and his face broke into the most incredibly winning smile. He said, "How you doing, you old pirate?"

The bald man with the computer bracket around his head saw that the situation was under control. He turned to the guards and pointed at the door behind them. The guards filed back with the bald man.

Holding Han at arm's length, Lando said, "So good to see you! I never thought I'd catch up with you again. Where you been?"

From the *Falcon*'s landing ramp, the golden droid observed, "Well, he seems very friendly."

Leia said, "Yes . . . very friendly." She followed close to C-3PO as he stepped away from the ramp, and couldn't help but think, *He's almost too friendly.*

"What are you doing here?" Lando asked Han.

"Ahh . . . repairs," Han said, indicating the *Falcon*. "I thought you could help me out."

Lando wore an expression of mild panic as he looked at the *Falcon* and said, "What have you done to my ship?"

"*Your* ship?" Han said, trying not to lose his cool. "Hey, remember, you lost her to me fair and square."

Lando grinned. Looking past Han, he caught the Wookiee's gaze. "And how are you doing, Chewbacca? You still hanging around with this loser?"

Chewbacca growled a reserved greeting and maintained his distance. Leia thought, *Chewie doesn't trust this guy either.*

Then Lando took sudden notice of the young woman who moved up behind Han with a protocol droid. Smiling at Leia, he said, "Hello. What have we here?" He moved close to her and said in his most engaging voice, "Welcome. I'm Lando Calrissian. I'm the administrator of this facility. And who might you be?"

"Leia."

"Welcome, Leia," Lando said with a bow; he then smoothly took Leia's left hand, cupped it in his own, and kissed the back of her glove.

Leia threw a desperate glance at Han. Returning her gaze to Lando, who still held her hand, she thought, *So much for gloves discouraging kisses.*

"All right, all right, you old smoothie," Han said as he took Leia's hand and steered her away from Lando.

Seeing Lando's now-empty hand, C-3PO stepped right up and took it. "Hello, sir. I am See-Threepio, Human Cyborg Relations. My facilities are at your —"

The protocol droid would have continued, but the still-smiling Lando had already released the mechanical hand and was walking after Han and Leia, who were moving down the walkway and heading for the door. Outraged, C-3PO exclaimed, "Well, really!" Then he noticed Chewbacca was also heading for the door, and started after him. C-3PO paused only briefly on the walkway to gaze at the city skyline. Cloud City was a very impressive sight, even to a droid.

Lando caught up alongside Han and asked, "What's wrong with the *Falcon*?"

"Hyperdrive."

"I'll get my people to work on it," Lando promised.

"Good," Han said.

Without breaking his stride, Lando turned to Leia and said, "You know, that ship saved my life quite a few times. She's the fastest hunk of junk in the galaxy."

"How's the gas mine?" Han asked, wanting to change the subject from his ship. "Is it still paying off for you?"

"Oh, not as well as I'd like," Lando admitted as they walked through the open doorway and proceeded through a white-walled corridor. "We're a small outpost and not very self-sufficient. And I've had supply problems of every kind. I've had labor difficulties. . . ."

Han laughed.

Lando asked, "What's so funny?"

"You," Han said. "Listen to you — you sound like a businessman, a responsible leader. Who'd have thought that, huh?"

Lando looked at Han and grinned. "You know, seeing you brings back a few things."

"Yeah," Han said, and tossed what he hoped was a reassuring glance to Leia, who was right behind him with Chewbacca and C-3PO.

"Yeah," Lando echoed. "I'm responsible these days. It's the price you pay for being successful."

Han and Lando laughed as the group passed a closed door on the corridor wall. C-3PO was walking right behind Chewbacca when the door slid open to reveal a silver-metal protocol droid. Despite its different color, the silver droid appeared to be the same model as C-3PO. C-3PO stopped in his tracks.

"Oh!" C-3PO said. "Nice to see a familiar face."

The silver droid glanced at the golden droid and mumbled, "E chu ta!" Then the silver droid stepped from the open doorway and brushed past.

"How rude!" C-3PO exclaimed as the droid walked off. C-3PO was about to turn and catch up with Chewbacca and the others when he heard a beeping sound come from the open doorway. Curious, C-3PO entered a narrow room, then heard another round of beeps from an adjoining chamber.

"That sounds like an Artoo unit in there," C-3PO said. "I wonder if . . ."

He followed the beeping noise into the next chamber, which had walls that were covered with pipes, gauges, and complex mechanisms. Not immediately seeing anyone, C-3PO called out, "Hello? Hello?" No response. Then he glanced around the room and commented, "How interesting."

"Who are you?" snapped a man's voice from the other side of the chamber.

C-3PO had to turn his head to face the speaker. And after he turned, he suddenly wished he had never entered the room. He tried to sound calm as he replied, "Who am I?" He wanted to get out immediately, and started to back up as he continued, "Oh, I'm terribly sorry. I . . . I didn't mean to intrude." He took a few more cautious steps backward and gestured pleadingly with his arms. "No, no, please don't get up." Then he threw his arms up defensively and cried, "No!"

There was a sudden explosion of blaster fire. A laser bolt slammed into C-3PO's chest. His upper torso smashed into the wall behind him and his head launched into the air. The rest of his body went everywhere else.

A smoldering gold metal foot and part of one leg clattered across the floor and skidded to a stop just shy of the doorway that remained opened to the corridor. The door slid shut a moment before Chewbacca —

having retraced his own steps — came back looking for C-3PO.

Chewbacca sniffed the air and smelled blaster fumes. Was that an unusual smell in a city that processed Tibanna gas for use in blasters? Chewbacca wasn't sure, but he did know that the protocol droid had been right behind him just a moment ago. So where had the droid gone?

The Wookiee growled. Something didn't smell right, and it wasn't just the scent of blasters. But since he couldn't see any sign of C-3PO, he turned and headed back down the corridor to rejoin his other friends.

It was night on Dagobah. R2-D2 was on top of the X-wing starfighter, moving into his socket behind the cockpit. Luke, wearing his orange g-suit, was loading a case onto the ship. Yoda stood on a nearby knoll and watched Luke. The Jedi Master didn't look happy.

"Luke!" Yoda said. "You must complete the training."

"I can't keep the vision out of my head," Luke replied as he hastily inspected his ship. "They're my friends. I've got to help them."

"You must not go!" Yoda insisted.

Luke faced Yoda and said, "But Han and Leia will die if I don't."

From out of the darkness, Ben Kenobi's voice spoke: "You don't know that."

To Luke's amazement, a slightly shimmering light began to glow in the air behind Yoda. Then the light materialized into the form of old Ben. The luminous Jedi wore a grave expression as he said, "Even Yoda cannot see their fate."

"But I can help them!" Luke argued. "I feel the Force!"

"But you cannot control it," Ben said. "This is a dangerous time for you, when you will be tempted by the dark side of the Force."

Yoda agreed, "Yes, yes. To Obi-Wan you listen. The cave. Remember your failure at the cave!"

"But I've learned so much since then, Master Yoda," Luke said as he returned his attention to his X-wing. "I promise to return and finish what I've begun. You have my word."

Ben explained, "It is you and your abilities the Emperor wants. That is why your friends are made to suffer."

"That's why I have to go," Luke said.

Ben said, "Luke, I don't want to lose you to the Emperor the way I lost Vader."

"You won't," Luke assured him. He thought back to his first meeting with Ben, back on Tatooine. Ben had told Luke that Darth Vader had been one of his pupils until he'd been seduced by the dark side of the Force. According to Ben, Vader had helped the Empire to destroy the Jedi Knights, including Luke's own father. *I'll never be anything like Darth Vader*, Luke thought. *And I won't be lost to the Emperor.*

Yoda said, "Stopped they must be. On this all depends. Only a fully trained Jedi Knight with the Force as his ally will conquer Vader and his Emperor." As Luke stowed the last of his gear onto the X-wing, Yoda continued, "If you end your training now, if you choose the quick and easy path, as Vader did, you will become an agent of evil."

"Patience," Ben said with great emphasis, as if it was the one word Luke should remember.

Patience? Luke couldn't believe anyone would encourage patience right now. Facing Ben, he snapped, "And sacrifice Han and Leia?"

Yoda answered, "If you honor what they fight for . . . yes!"

Luke reached for the lower rung of the X-wing's retractable ladder and looked away from Ben and Yoda.

Ben said, "If you choose to face Vader, you will do it alone. I cannot interfere."

"I understand," Luke muttered. Then he climbed the ladder to the starfighter's open cockpit and said, "Artoo, fire up the converters."

As the X-wing's engines fired up, Ben warned, "Luke, don't give in to hate — that leads to the dark side."

"Strong is Vader," Yoda added. "Mind what you have learned. Save you it can."

"I will," Luke said as he pulled on his helmet. "And I'll return. I promise." The cockpit canopy lowered, and the X-wing lifted off from the ground and ascended into the night sky.

As Yoda raised his gaze to watch the departing X-wing, Ben's apparition faded into the darkness. Yoda sighed, looked down at the ground, and shook his head sadly. "Told you, I did," he said. "Reckless is he. Now matters are worse."

Ben's disembodied voice said, "That boy is our last hope."

Yoda returned his gaze to the sky and said mysteriously, "No. There is another."

CHAPTER 14

Leia paced before the wide window that offered a magnificent view of Cloud City. She was within the living quarters that had been assigned to her and she wore fresh clothes, all courtesy of Lando Calrissian. From the skylight that dominated the circular room's ceiling, natural light poured in and illuminated the interior and its comfortable furnishings. The entire room and all its contents were white and immaculately clean.

Leia didn't like the place one bit.

The room's main door slid open and Han entered. "The ship's almost finished," he said as Leia crossed the room to him. "Two or three more things and we're in great shape."

"The sooner the better," Leia said. "Something's wrong here. No one has seen or knows anything about Threepio. He's been gone too long to have gotten lost."

"Relax," Han said. He took Leia by the shoulders and gently kissed her forehead. "I'll talk to Lando. See what I can find out."

"I don't trust Lando." Leia pulled away from Han and sat on a plush white couch.

"Well, I don't trust him, either," Han said as he sat down beside Leia. "But he is my friend. Besides, we'll soon be gone."

Trying to keep the sadness from her voice, Leia said, "And then you're as good as gone, aren't you?"

Han looked away, then looked back to Leia's troubled face. He didn't know how to respond to her question, so he just gazed into her eyes and remained silent.

Like any large metropolis, Cloud City had to deal with unwanted junk. But because Cloud City was not built upon solid ground and had no land-based natural resources, dumping was not an economical option. Virtually everything — from outmoded technology to broken appliances — was recycled into usable materials. And the recycling process began in the junk rooms.

Chewbacca found the junk rooms on a level below Lando Calrissian's headquarters. The Wookiee had already visited every other accessible part of the building. He was determined to find C-3PO. As

Chewbacca entered a junk room and saw the piles of scrap metal that were heaped throughout, he wished C-3PO hadn't wound up here, of all places. But where else could C-3PO be?

Chewbacca made his way past the scrap heaps, keeping his eyes peeled for gold-plated metal. He picked up several pieces, but nothing was from a protocol droid. He tossed the scraps aside and kept searching.

Then he heard a roar. Not an animal sound, but a noise made by intense fire.

Chewbacca edged around a high stack of crushed metal and found a conveyer that moved scrap from a garbage chute to the other side of the room. Four small, porcine humanoids — Chewbacca recognized them as Ugnaughts — were stationed on both sides of the long conveyer, from which they selectively removed valuable scrap. Anything the Ugnaughts didn't want was fed through an open oval-shaped door into a blazing furnace, the source of the roaring sound.

Chewbacca sighted a flash of gold on the conveyer and realized he was looking at the blaster-scorched remains of C-3PO. The Wookiee pushed his way past the scrap heaps and Ugnaughts to grab C-3PO's headless torso. Then he quickly knocked the droid's other dismembered parts off the conveyer.

One of the Ugnaughts had seized C-3PO's head.

Chewbacca barked a command at the Ugnaught, but rather than hand over the head, the Ugnaught tossed it to one of his fellow workers. Chewbacca tried to intercept the catch but missed, and failed to prevent the droid's head from being thrown to another Ugnaught. That Ugnaught threw it to another, who missed, and C-3PO's head clattered against the floor.

Chewbacca howled with rage. And the Ugnaughts quickly learned the hard way that it's pure foolishness to play keep-away with a Wookiee.

Leia and Han were still in the bright white living quarters when Chewbacca entered, carrying a packing case. The case was crammed with C-3PO's parts.

"What happened?" Leia gasped, rising from the couch.

Chewbacca set the case onto the circular table at the center of the room, then grunted an explanation.

"Where?" Han said.

Chewbacca repeated himself.

Han said, "Found him in a junk pile?"

Leia shook her head as she peered into the case. "Oh, what a mess. Chewie, do you think you can repair him?"

Chewbacca examined some of C-3PO's pieces, looked at Leia, then shrugged.

Han said, "Lando's got people who can fix him."

"No, thanks," Leia said, a bit surprised that Han had even considered the idea. From what she'd seen so far, Lando dealt with most of his responsibilities through his aide Lobot, the bald cyborg with the cranial computer bracket. According to Lando, Lobot's headband kept in constant contact with Cloud City's central computer. She had as much reason to trust Lobot as she did Lando, which was not at all.

Just then, an electronic chime sounded and Lando stepped down into the room. Standing in the doorway, he said, "I'm sorry. Am I interrupting something?"

"Not really," Leia said.

Lando cast a long, appreciative glance at Leia, then beamed and said, "You look absolutely beautiful. You truly belong here with us among the clouds."

"Thank you," Leia said coolly, thinking, *I wonder how many times he's used that line.*

Lando said, "Will you join me for a little refreshment?"

Han looked at Lando suspiciously. Chewbacca answered with a hungry bark.

Lando added, "Everyone's invited, of course." He offered his hand to Leia, but Han stepped in and Leia took his arm. Lando was turning to lead them out of the room when he noticed the gold-metal limbs in the case on the table. With a quizzical expression, Lando said, "Having trouble with your droid?"

Leia and Han exchanged a quick glance, then Han looked at Lando and said, "No. No problem. Why?"

Han and Leia exited the room, and Lando and Chewbacca followed, leaving C-3PO's parts behind. The group proceeded into a window-lined corridor, where long shafts of light fell across white walls and columns. As they walked past a group of uniformed laborers, Lando gestured at the surroundings and said, "So, you see, since we're a small operation, we don't fall into the . . . uh . . . jurisdiction of the Empire."

Leia said, "So you're part of the mining guild, then?"

"No, not actually," Lando said, leading the way down another corridor. "Our operation is small enough not to be noticed . . . which is advantageous for everybody, since our customers are anxious to avoid attracting attention to themselves."

Han asked, "Aren't you afraid the Empire's going to find out about this little operation and shut you down?"

"That's always been a danger looming like a shadow over everything we've built here," Lando said as he approached a closed pair of doors, "but things have developed that will ensure security." Chewbacca sniffed the air and growled. That rotten smell again.

Lando stopped at the double doors and said, "I've just made a deal that will keep the Empire out of here forever."

The doors parted at the middle and slid sideways into the wall to reveal a white-walled dining room with a long, neatly arranged banquet table. At the far end of the table, rising from his seat, was Darth Vader.

Chewbacca roared. Leia froze. And Solo made his move, quick-drawing his blaster pistol to fire at Vader. But the dark lord, moving with incredible speed, raised his right black-gloved hand and deflected the fired bolt into the wall. Han rapidly squeezed off three more shots, but all were just as easily nullified by Vader. Then Han felt an invisible tug as his blaster was torn from his grip. The weapon flew through the air, straight at Vader, who caught it by the barrel.

Facing Leia and her allies, Vader lowered the blaster to the table and said, "We would be honored if you would join us."

A figure stepped out from an alcove behind Vader. It was Boba Fett. Clutching his blaster rifle across his armored chest, the masked bounty hunter moved so he was just off to Vader's left side.

Leia, Han, and Chewbacca were still standing in the open doorway when they heard a clattering of footsteps behind them. A squad of blaster-wielding stormtroopers had taken up position outside the dining room. Near them stood Lobot, who was unarmed.

Even though Leia had already expressed her mistrust for Lando, and heard his talk of deals that would keep the Empire out of Cloud City, it was only upon seeing Lobot with the stormtroopers that she realized . . . *Lando set us up!*

She looked at Lando, as did Han and Chewbacca. Lando looked Han square in the eye and said grimly, "I had no choice. They arrived right before you did. I'm sorry."

"I'm sorry, too," Han said, his expression blank. He took Leia's arm, and together they turned, stepped toward the banquet table, and faced Darth Vader. After all, there was nowhere else to go. Then Chewbacca and Lando entered the dining room, and the double doors slid closed behind them.

Luke's X-wing starfighter raced across space. Although no one had told him the location of his friends, his vision had been crystal clear. They were in a city in the clouds. He was certain he would find them on Bespin.

Through his cockpit window, Luke sighted the giant gaseous planet in the distance. Behind him, R2-D2 beeped and whistled. Luke consulted the scope that displayed the translation for the astromech's language, then answered, "No. Threepio's with them."

Sounding more distressed, R2-D2 whistled again.

"Just hang on," Luke said. "We're almost there."

Luke couldn't stop thinking about his vision, how his friends were in pain. He accelerated toward Bespin and hoped he would arrive in time to help them.

CHAPTER 15

Chewbacca was in agony.

The Wookiee was in a Cloud City prison cell and a high-pitched siren was screeching and echoing off the cell's durasteel walls. He pressed both hands hard against the sides of his hairy head, trying in vain to protect his sensitive ears. He felt like his skull was about to split wide open.

Chewbacca started pacing back and forth within the large cell, his arms flailing in useless effort to ward off the violent din. Desperate to escape, he reached up to grab the thick, black metal bars that crisscrossed overhead and separated him from the upper ceiling. He tugged at the bars but they wouldn't yield. Suddenly, the siren ended, but it took Chewbacca a moment to comprehend it was over. The noise was still ringing in his ears.

The Wookiee shook his head and moaned, waiting for the pain to drain off. Exhausted, he looked down to a metal bench, on which rested the case that contained C-3PO's parts. Who had taken the case from Leia's living quarters and delivered it to his cell? Why hadn't the stormtroopers just returned the parts to the Cloud City junk room? Chewbacca had no idea. He was more relieved that the parts hadn't been smelted than curious about how they'd arrived in the cell. And now that the siren was silenced, he could concentrate on reassembling the droid.

He reached into the case and removed one of C-3PO's hands, then set the hand aside and picked up the droid's head. He contemplated it for a moment, looking into the droid's dead eyes as if they held some secret. Without any tools at his disposal, Chewbacca doubted he could do much for the droid. But he could try.

He reached for the droid's torso and placed it on his lap. Then he examined the scorched metal at the bottom of the head and found the neck ring was unbroken. He stuck C-3PO's head into the torso's neck socket and began to reconnect the wires and adjust the circuits.

The lights in C-3PO's eyes sparked on and then flickered out. Chewbacca made another adjustment and the eyes switched on again. This was followed by a flurry of almost unintelligible words, uttered at varying speeds and tones, from C-3PO's mouth: "Mmm. Oh, my. Uh, I, uh — Take this off, uh, don't mean to intrude here. I, don't, no, no, no . . . please don't get up. No!"

Chewbacca twisted a wire and C-3PO's eyes switched off. Then he squeezed a circuit as he pulled a wire, and the eyes illuminated again. But this time, C-3PO's head moved from side to side in the torso's neck socket and the droid spoke clearly: "Stormtroopers? Here? We're in danger. I must tell the others."

Then C-3PO tried to move, and realized the awful truth. "Oh, no!" he cried. "I've been shot!"

Darth Vader watched as two stormtroopers prepared an elaborate mechanism in the prison entry area. The mechanism consisted of an adjustable rack that stood vertically and faced a slanted panel of assorted instruments, including chemical injectors, microsurgical vibroscalpels, diagnostic scanners, and an electroshock assembly. All the instruments were designed to induce pain, which was appropriate since the mechanism was engineered for torture.

Han Solo was strapped to the rack. Unable to move his arms or legs, he studied the pain-inducing instruments on the facing panel and tried to brace himself for the worst. From what he'd heard about

Imperial torture devices, the diagnostic scanners would be used to anticipate loss of consciousness and the chemical injectors would keep him awake. That way, he wouldn't pass out, and would experience every measure of pain.

Darth Vader walked around the instrument panel and stood close to Han. Because the rack elevated Han's body, Vader had to tilt his own head back slightly to stare directly — through the lenses of his black helmet — into Han's eyes. Han glared at Vader and clenched his bound fists.

A red light illuminated on the slanted panel, and the rack tilted forward. Han's head and neck were not restrained, so he twisted his face away and squeezed his eyes shut as the rack lowered his upper body into direct contact with the horrendous instruments. Vader leaned in closer and watched Han's facial responses with interest.

A spark flashed at the top of the instrument panel, and Han winced.

A second spark flashed, and Han screamed. The pain was overwhelming.

The third spark came, and Han learned there was pain beyond overwhelming.

Han didn't pass out. And the torture mechanism was just getting started.

*   *   *

Solo's piercing cries filtered through the closed door that separated the prison entry area from the holding chamber. In the holding chamber, the closed door was guarded by two stormtroopers. Lando Calrissian and Lobot stood a short distance from the stormtroopers, as did Boba Fett. Hearing Han's screams, Lando and Boba Fett slowly turned to look at each other. Lando tried to keep his face as expressionless as Fett's helmet.

The door slid open. Darth Vader ducked his head as he strode through the doorway and entered the holding chamber.

Lando said, "Lord Vader."

Brushing past Lando, Vader stopped to face Fett and said, "You may take Captain Solo to Jabba the Hutt after I have Skywalker." Then he walked off.

"He's no good to me dead," Boba Fett said, following Vader into a corridor with Lando and Lobot in their wake.

"He will not be permanently damaged," Vader assured him, passing two stormtroopers as he entered an open lift tube.

"Lord Vader," Lando repeated. "What about Leia and the Wookiee?"

Turning to face Lando, who stood just outside the lift tube, Vader said, "They must never again leave this city."

Lando was stunned. "That was never a condition of our agreement, nor was giving Han to this bounty hunter!"

"Perhaps you think you're being treated unfairly," Vader said.

Lando knew there was only one answer he could give. "No," he said.

"Good," Vader replied. "It would be unfortunate if I had to leave a garrison here." The lift tube door slid shut.

Boba Fett turned and headed back to the holding chamber, leaving Lando and Lobot standing in the corridor near the lift tube. Watching Boba walk away, Lando muttered, "This deal is getting worse all the time."

In the large cell, working without tools, Chewbacca had managed to make some progress with C-3PO. More wires had been sorted, some had been reconnected, and the droid's right arm — like his head — had been reattached to his upper torso. Chewbacca had the torso propped up on his lap as he adjusted the circuits that were housed in the middle of the droid's back. C-3PO's audio and visual sensors seemed to be working fine and, as he faced the cell's far wall, he was able to comment on the Wookiee's handiwork.

"Oh, yes, that's very good," C-3PO said as the Wookiee tweaked a circuit. "I like that." Suddenly, the lights in the protocol droid's eyes flashed off. "Oh! Something's not right because now I can't see." After Chewbacca made another adjustment, C-3PO continued, "Oh. Oh, that's much better."

Then C-3PO tried to wiggle the fingers on his right hand, but something about the action felt awkward. "Wait," he said, and twisted his head to look down at his chest. "Wait! Oh, my!" he cried. Where he'd expected to see his chest, he instead saw the exposed circuits on his back, and was suddenly livid. "What have you done? I'm backward, you flea-bitten furball. Only an overgrown mophead like you would be stupid enough —"

Chewbacca threw the circuit breaker at the base of C-3PO's neck, and the droid's eyes and voice switched off. The Wookiee was about to resume the repairs when he smelled something in the air, then heard the sound of approaching footsteps. As he placed C-3PO's upper body with the rest of his parts, the cell's door slid up into the ceiling. Turning to the doorway, he watched as two stormtroopers hauled in Han.

Han's arms were draped over the stormtroopers' shoulders. His eyes were open, his jaw hung loose, and the toes of his boots dragged along the floor behind him. The troopers dumped him into the cell and left, sealing the door behind them.

Chewbacca barked with concern as he kneeled down to hug Han.

"I feel terrible," Han mumbled.

The Wookiee gently lifted Han to his feet, then helped him over to a bare metal slab, a retractable resting platform that projected from the wall. Han winced as Chewbacca lowered his aching body upon the slab.

A second door slid open, and two stormtroopers shoved Princess Leia into the cell. Instead of the clothes that Lando had given her, she was back in the same insulated jumpsuit she'd worn when she'd arrived at Cloud City. She saw Chewbacca standing beside Han's prone form. Chewbacca whimpered a sad greeting.

Leia moved to the metal slab, then knelt beside Han and gently pushed her fingers through his hair. His eyes briefly locked on hers. She said, "Why are they doing this?"

"They never even asked me any questions," Han said.

Leia kissed his forehead. Then the door slid open behind her. Leia turned to see two blue-uniformed Cloud City guards enter, followed by Calrissian.

At the sight of the caped man, Chewbacca roared.

Han was having difficulty raising his head, so Leia

turned back to him and whispered, "Lando." She remained beside Han as Lando and the two guards walked to the center of the cell. Leia noticed Lando wasn't wearing his customary smile, and that his expression was downright grim. But after the way he'd handed them over to Darth Vader, she didn't much care whether Cloud City's administrator was having a bad day.

Han struggled to rise from the slab and said, "Get out of here, Lando!"

"Shut up and listen!" Lando shouted. "Now, Vader has agreed to turn Leia and Chewie over to me."

"Over to you?" Han said with disbelief.

Leia wondered, *What's Lando trying to pull this time?*

Lando said, "They'll have to stay here, but at least they'll be safe."

"What about Han?" Leia asked.

"Vader's giving him to the bounty hunter," Lando said.

Leia glared at Lando. "Vader wants us all dead!"

"He doesn't want you at all," Lando said. "He's after somebody called, uh . . ." Lando had to search his memory for the name Vader had said in the holding chamber, but quickly remembered. ". . . Skywalker."

"Luke?" Han said, sitting up on the slab.

"Lord Vader has set a trap for him," Lando said.

"And we're the bait," Leia immediately concluded.

Lando said, "Yeah, well, he's on his way."

"Perfect," Han said as he slowly rose to his feet. On shaky legs, he stepped toward Lando and said, "You fixed us all real good, didn't you? My friend!"

Han moved fast for a man who'd just come off an Imperial torture rack. His right fist connected with Lando's jaw, sending Lando stumbling back into one of his guards. But Han's coordination and sense of balance were all off, and he tried to grab Lando as he fell forward. He only managed to snare Lando's cape before he hit the floor.

There wasn't any trouble with the guards' coordination. Han tried to push himself up from the floor, but one guard drew a blaster and slammed the weapon's butt into Han's back. The other guard drew his blaster and aimed it at Chewbacca. The Wookiee roared and Lando shouted, "Stop!"

The guards held their fire and Leia moved beside Han's fallen form. Lando pulled his cape back around his shoulders and said, "I've done all I can. I'm sorry I couldn't do better, but I got my own problems."

Han looked up from the floor and sneered, "Yeah, you're a real hero."

Lando, looking more grim than ever, walked out of the cell with his two guards. After the door slid shut, Chewbacca knelt down beside Han. As Han caught his breath, Leia shook her head and said, "You certainly have a way with people."

Han tried to offer a smile, but after everything he'd been through, even smiling hurt.

Even without Darth Vader's sinister presence, the windowless carbon-freezing chamber was among the least inviting places on Cloud City. The dark chamber was an effective but inelegant device, used to mix Tibanna gas with carbonite, then flash-freeze the mixture into solid blocks that could be easily transported. The mixing and freezing were done in a deep pit at the center of an elevated circular platform that dominated the chamber, and the carbonite blocks were removed by retrieval tongs — large retractable manipulator claws — that were housed in the high ceiling above the central pit.

Steam blasted and billowed from various vents throughout the chamber, which was ringed by a narrow catwalk. Two stairways descended from the catwalk to the elevated platform's surface: a concentric design of embedded red lights, air intakes, and black metal. The combination of the red-illuminated metal floor and rising steam made the platform resemble an immense heating element that was set on "hot." If the chamber's inhospitable design were not enough to discourage tourism, the platform's perimeter was also without a guardrail.

Darth Vader stood at the platform's edge, gazing down at the sheer drop to the metal pipes and hoses that laced across the chamber floor. He turned and walked through rising steam to the platform's center, where Lando, Lobot, and two stormtroopers stood near the open pit. In the pit, two Ugnaughts busily readied the control casing for the mixing and freezing process.

Vader said, "This facility is crude, but it should be adequate to freeze Skywalker for his journey to the Emperor."

An Imperial soldier stepped onto the platform and approached the dark lord. "Lord Vader," said the soldier, "ship approaching, X-wing class."

"Good," Vader said. There were many carbon-freezing chambers on Cloud City, but Vader had chosen this one for its strategic position: It had the advantage of being closest to Platform 327, where the *Millennium Falcon* would be easily sighted by Skywalker. Confident that Luke would walk right into his trap, Vader ordered, "Monitor Skywalker and allow him to land."

The soldier nodded, then walked quickly from the platform.

Lando said, "Lord Vader, we only use this facility for carbon freezing. You put him in there . . . it might kill him."

"I do not want the Emperor's prize damaged," Vader said. "We will test it . . . on Captain Solo."

Vader moved across the platform, and the two stormtroopers followed. As they passed by Lobot and Lando, one stormtrooper gave Lando a mild shove to stand aside.

Understandably, Lando didn't shove back.

In his X-wing starfighter, Luke descended through Bespin's upper atmosphere. Behind him, R2-D2 beeped with excitement as the X-wing flew through beautiful white clouds and emerged within visual range of a great, floating metropolis.

Cloud City was straight ahead.

CHAPTER 16

Boba Fett led the procession along the catwalk that wrapped around the wall of the carbon-freezing chamber. The sinister bounty hunter was followed by Han Solo, whose hands were manacled before him, then Princess Leia and Chewbacca. Strapped to the Wookiee's back, a cargo net carried C-3PO's parts. The droid was upset that only his head and right arm had been reattached, and seemed even more dismayed that his head faced the opposite direction of Chewbacca's. In this manner of travel, the droid was unable to see where they were going, and was forced to face the two stormtroopers who followed the Wookiee.

C-3PO saw more stormtroopers stationed around the chamber, and tried to twist his head around to see where Chewbacca was heading. "If only you had attached my legs, I wouldn't be in this ridiculous position," the droid complained. "Now, remember,

Chewbacca, you have a responsibility to me, so don't do anything foolish."

The group followed Fett down the stairs to the chamber's elevated platform. On the way down, Leia noticed Lobot standing at the bottom of the stairway. Then she saw Lando, standing near the platform's center, looking down into a pit where some Ugnaughts were working.

Two stormtroopers preceded Darth Vader into the chamber via the second stairway. As Vader descended to the elevated platform, he saw that the Ugnaughts were making final adjustments to the control casing into the central pit. It appeared the carbon-freezing apparatus was all in place.

Han came to a stop behind Lando and said, "What's going on . . . buddy?"

Without turning to face Han, Lando said, "You're being put into carbon freeze."

Leia and Han were standing just a short distance apart, but when they turned to face each other, Leia felt the distance like a chasm. Across from them, Fett approached Vader and said, "What if he doesn't survive? He's worth a lot to me."

"The Empire will compensate you if he dies," Vader said. Then he turned to the stormtroopers and commanded, "Put him in!"

Realizing what was about to happen, Chewbacca let out a wild howl. He threw his right arm out to his side, striking a stormtrooper with enough force to launch the figure from the elevated platform. Before anyone thought to react, Chewbacca lashed out with his left arm and disposed of a second stormtrooper in the same fashion. Across the platform, Boba Fett brought up his blaster rifle, but Vader — hoping to preserve his other captives — lashed out and grabbed the rifle's barrel, forcing the bounty hunter to aim away from the melee.

"Oh, no!" C-3PO cried from Chewbacca's back as more stormtroopers rushed the Wookiee. "No, no, no! Stop!"

"Stop, Chewie, stop!" Han shouted. "Stop!"

Chewbacca threw a third stormtrooper from the platform.

Glad to have Han's support for once, C-3PO pleaded, "Yes, stop, please! I'm not ready to die."

Han shouted louder, "Hey, hey! Listen to me. Chewie!"

Chewbacca howled. The stormtroopers swarmed around the Wookiee, trying to fit a pair of durasteel binders over his thick wrists in case he attacked again. Still enraged, the Wookiee was considering falling back over the side of the platform and dragging as many stormtroopers as he could with him when Han said, "Chewie, this won't help me."

Realizing the Wookiee was still considering doing something drastic, Han shouted, "Hey!" He gave

Chewbacca a stern look. "Save your strength. There'll be another time. The princess — you have to take care of her."

Leia glanced at Darth Vader and Boba Fett, then edged past the stormtroopers to stand close between Chewbacca and Han.

Han looked up at Chewbacca and said, "You hear me? Huh?"

Whimpering, Chewbacca nodded. As the stormtroopers secured the binders to the Wookiee's wrists, Leia and Han looked sorrowfully at each other. Both knew it might be their last moment together. Han moved forward and Leia raised her mouth to his for one final kiss.

The stormtroopers pulled Han away and made him walk backward until he stood upon a hydraulic lift at the platform's center. Han kept his eyes on Leia.

Leia called out, "I love you!"

To which Han said, "I know."

Two Ugnaughts approached Han, removed the manacles from his wrists, then stepped away from him. Leia watched the lift descend, carrying Han down into the central pit. From where Leia stood, only Han's head was visible. His gaze never strayed from her.

Lando looked from Han to Leia, then back to Han. Chewbacca howled.

Darth Vader gestured to an Ugnaught at a nearby control panel. The Ugnaught threw a switch, and only then did Han look away, flinching once before he appeared to vanish within a powerful blast of steam that exploded from the pit.

From behind Chewbacca, C-3PO said, "What . . . what's going on? Turn around. Chewbacca, I can't see."

Chewbacca whimpered. The steam was still clearing as the large retrieval tongs descended from the ceiling to the pit. The tongs locked onto the solid block of carbonite, then raised the heavy block from the pit to the platform.

Colored a lustrous dark gray, the carbonite block was 81 centimeters wide, 203 centimeters high, and 25 centimeters deep. It weighed over 100 kilograms, not including the weight of Han Solo, who was frozen solid within it. His face and the front of his body protruded slightly from the block's flat surface, with sharp, clearly defined creases on his shirt and pants. His hands and forearms — raised defensively — protruded the most. In all, he had the appearance of an unfinished statue, its form only partially emerged from a slab of black metal. But in this case, the statue looked as if it had been fighting to escape.

Two Ugnaughts stepped up to inspect the carbonite block's control casing, a frame with slender monitors embedded in its sides. After checking the monitors for gas ratio and carbonite integrity, one Ugnaught reached up to place his small, strong hands against the block's front, then pushed. The block fell back against the metal platform with a loud clang, and the noise made Leia jump back against Chewbacca.

But she couldn't tear her gaze from Han's frozen form, which now faced the ceiling. Prone on the floor with his hands clutching at the air, Han looked as if he were perpetually drowning. Devastated, Leia shuddered, and Chewbacca turned his body to her.

The Wookiee's movement allowed a very curious C-3PO to finally get a glimpse of what had transpired. From Chewbacca's back, the dismembered droid said, "Oh . . . they've encased him in carbonite. He should be quite well protected — if he survived the freezing process, that is."

While Fett and Vader watched, Lando stepped over to the prone block, knelt beside it, and examined the control casing's monitor for life systems. He pushed a button, listened to the monitor, then checked the illuminated readout.

Vader said, "Well, Calrissian, did he survive?"

"Yes, he's alive," Lando replied. "And in perfect hibernation."

As Lando rose and stepped away from the carbonite block, Vader turned to Boba Fett and said, "He's all yours, bounty hunter."

Fett responded with a single nod.

Vader looked to the Ugnaughts and ordered, "Reset the chamber for Skywalker."

Just then, an Imperial officer descended to the chamber platform. Stopping in front of Vader, he said, "Skywalker has just landed, my lord."

"Good," Vader said. "See to it that he finds his way in here."

The officer hurried out. Vader turned and watched Lando approach Leia and attempt to take her arm, apparently with the hope she would allow him to escort her from the chamber. Leia jerked her arm away.

Vader said, "Calrissian, take the princess and the Wookiee to my ship."

Lando was outraged. "You said they'd be left in the city under my supervision."

"I am altering the deal," Vader said. "Pray I don't alter it any further."

As Vader swept out of the carbon-freezing chamber, Lando's hand instinctively went to his throat. He knew what Vader would do to him if he pushed his luck.

Lando looked at Lobot. Lobot returned the gaze with a sidelong glance. And with that single, silent communication, Lobot knew what he had to do.

Luke had landed his X-wing starfighter without any difficulty, but as he and R2-D2 moved carefully down a white-walled, high-ceilinged corridor, he knew that something was very wrong on Cloud City. He didn't understand why there hadn't been anyone to greet or confront him on the landing platform.

Where is everybody?

Moving quietly forward, Luke arrived at a side hallway. He peered around the corner to see that the hallway connected with another corridor. He was about to enter the hallway when he heard footsteps.

Luke pulled back quickly, drew his blaster pistol, and flattened against the wall. With his blaster held tight in his right hand, he leaned forward, took a cautious peek down the hallway, and saw Boba Fett walking down the corridor.

Boba Fett?! What's that bounty hunter doing here? He saw Boba Fett's helmet shift slightly, as if he were about to turn to face Luke, but he didn't turn his head as he kept walking. Then Luke remembered the bounty on Han. *Maybe Yoda and Ben were wrong. Maybe my vision had nothing to do with Darth Vader and the Emperor. Maybe it was all about Boba Fett capturing Han.*

Fett was followed by a floating slab of metal that Luke couldn't make out. The floating slab was followed by two blue-uniformed Cloud City guards, who held the end of the slab and appeared to be guiding it through the hallway. Luke realized the slab was resting on a thin repulsor sled, an antigravity device used to transport heavy objects. The guards were followed by a pair of Imperial stormtroopers.

Stormtroopers! Luke suddenly realized that the Empire was definitely involved with whatever was going on at Cloud City. *Looks like Ben and Yoda were right.*

The procession passed out of Luke's viewing range. Keeping his blaster out, Luke moved quickly down the hallway until he'd arrived at the next corridor. Peering around the corner, he saw the end of the procession — the backs of the departing stormtroopers — just before they rounded a corner and he lost sight of them again.

R2-D2 had followed Luke through the hallway, and beeped as he arrived at his master's side. Luke raised a hand, signaling the droid to be silent and stay put. R2-D2 obediently stopped beeping and rolled back from him.

Trusting that the procession was now far enough ahead of him that he could follow unnoticed, Luke stepped forward into the corridor. Which was a mistake.

Boba was positioned near the same corner where Luke had lost sight of the two stormtroopers. The bounty hunter's blaster rifle was aimed at Luke. Boba fired.

Luke fell back into the hallway as the laser bolt whizzed past him and impacted at the hallway wall.

He realized too late that he must have been spotted by Fett's targeting rangefinder as the hunter had led the others past the hallway. Fett quickly fired two more bolts, which smashed into the corridor wall near Luke's position, then fired a fourth bolt that followed the first into the hallway wall.

Leia was walking down a corridor with Chewbacca and C-3PO — the droid's pieces still strapped to the Wookiee's back — when she heard four blaster shots. The shots sounded like they'd come from behind, so Leia looked back, but all she saw were two of the four stormtroopers in her escort. The other two were in front of her, and in the lead were a gray-uniformed Imperial lieutenant and Lando Calrissian.

Lando heard the fired blasters, too. He continued walking without missing a step but adjusted his cape slightly so neither the lieutenant nor anyone behind him was able to see what he did next. With his left hand, Lando reached to a thin comlink that was strapped to his right wrist, tapped a key sequence, and sent a signal to Lobot.

R2-D2 beeped frantically. Luke patted R2-D2's dome, trying to reassure the astromech that he'd be all right. Around the corner from Luke, the two shots that had struck the corridor wall had left smoldering scorch marks.

Luke held his blaster pistol and edged out into the corridor. *No sign of Fett.* He pressed forward, trying to pick up the bounty hunter's trail.

As Luke approached another side hallway, he heard more footsteps. He passed a window as he entered the hallway and did not consider that the light from the window might cast his shadow onto the hallway's wall.

The Imperial lieutenant was walking just behind Calrissian when he saw a shadow glide across the wall of an adjoining hallway. The lieutenant stopped, gestured at Lando to open a nearby door, then signaled the stormtroopers under his command. As the stormtroopers took up firing position, the lieutenant grabbed Princess Leia and yanked her after Lando.

Luke jumped back against the hallway wall as the waiting stormtroopers fired their blaster rifles at him. After several laser bolts whizzed past him, he risked a quick glance up the hall and was almost overwhelmed by what he saw.

Four stormtroopers. Chewbacca and Leia! That Imperial officer's holding Leia like a body shield! Is that C-3PO on Chewie's back? Who's the caped man opening that door?

The stormtroopers kept shooting at him, but Luke held his fire and watched as the caped man stepped

through the open doorway. As three of the stormtroopers shoved Chewbacca through the doorway,
Leia saw Luke and shouted, "Luke! Luke, don't — it's
a trap!"

The Imperial officer dragged Leia after Chewbacca, but Leia gripped the doorway and shouted
again, "It's a trap!" Then Leia was pulled through.
One stormtrooper fired two more shots at Luke, then
exited the same way as the others.

The doorway remained open.

So it's a trap, Luke thought. *But what happens to
my friends if I don't try to rescue them?*

Luke headed for the open doorway.

CHAPTER 17

His blaster pistol at the ready, Luke stepped through the open doorway and into a dark antechamber. R2-D2 tried to follow, but a moment after Luke entered, the door slid down and locked behind him, leaving the little droid in the outer corridor.

There wasn't any sign of Luke's friends or the stormtroopers in the antechamber. Except for the locked door behind Luke, the only visible exit was an open lift tube. The lift's floor was circular, and only large enough to carry a single passenger.

Luke stepped onto the lift, and was instantly transported up through a hole in the ceiling. He'd been delivered to the top of an elevated platform in a large chamber. There was steam everywhere. Luke looked around at the pipes and hoses that lined the walls and ceiling, and he tried to determine the chamber's function. As he stepped off the lift, a metal grate slid over the lift and locked in place.

Luke realized an unseen enemy was controlling his movements, drawing him into a predetermined path and sealing off his avenues of retreat. He looked at his blaster pistol. *How effective will a blaster be against someone I can't even see?* Uncertain of where to proceed, he kept his blaster drawn as he moved away from the sealed lift.

"The Force is with you, young Skywalker," a deep voice rumbled from behind him, causing Luke to turn fast. "But you are not a Jedi yet."

It was Darth Vader.

The dark lord was positioned above Luke, standing on a grated floor that was connected to the elevated platform by a stairway. Luke holstered his blaster as he climbed the steps to stand before Vader, then drew his lightsaber and ignited its blue blade.

Vader activated his own red-bladed lightsaber. Luke stepped forward and raised his weapon. There was a mild electrical crackling sound as the two men crossed sabers.

Luke swung first, but Vader blocked the blow with ease. Luke pulled away and swung again, but Vader blocked and pushed back with considerable strength, knocking Luke to the floor. Keeping his lightsaber angled up toward Vader, Luke rose to his feet and assumed a defensive position. Vader swung at Luke, but Luke blocked and swung back, and soon their lightsabers were sweeping and clashing faster than the eye could follow.

The duel had just begun.

What's happening to Luke? Leia wondered. She and the droid-toting Wookiee were being led through yet another corridor, with two stormtroopers behind them, two in front, and Lando and the Imperial lieutenant back in the lead. Glancing at the back of Lando's head, she swore, *If I ever get out of this, I'll fix Lando so he never smiles again.*

As the group proceeded past an intersection in the corridor, Leia glanced to her right and saw Lobot approaching with a group of Cloud City guards from a connecting hallway. To her surprise, more guards suddenly materialized from adjoining hallways, then drew and aimed their sleek blaster pistols at the Imperial lieutenant and stormtroopers. Outnumbered and unprepared, the stormtroopers raised their armored arms and held out their blaster rifles in surrender.

Lando shoved the Imperial lieutenant toward one of the guards, then turned to the two stormtroopers behind them and took their weapons. Leia gaped as Lando stepped past her and handed both blaster rifles to Lobot.

"Well done," Lando said to his aide, then turned to the two stormtroopers behind Leia and Chewbacca and took away their blaster rifles. Turning back to Lobot, Lando said, "Hold them in the security tower — and keep it quiet. Move."

As Lobot and the Cloud City guards escorted their Imperial captives out of the corridor, Lando handed the two blaster rifles to Leia, then turned his attention to the binders that were locked around Chewbacca's wrists.

Surprised by this turn of events, Leia asked Lando, "What do you think you're doing?"

"We're getting out of here," Lando replied.

From the net at Chewbacca's back, C-3PO chimed in, "I knew all along it had to be a mistake."

The moment Chewbacca's binders were unlocked, he reached out and wrapped his hairy fingers around Lando's neck. Leia glared at Lando and said, "Do you think that after what you did to Han we're going to trust you?"

"I had no choice. . . ." Lando gasped.

"What are you doing?" C-3PO cried, twisting at Chewbacca's back in a desperate effort to see the others. "Trust him, trust him!"

Leia said, "Oh, so we understand, don't we, Chewie? He had no choice."

Chewbacca tightened his grip on Lando and leaned forward, forcing Lando to his knees. Lando's voice was a choked whisper: "I'm just trying to help —"

"We don't need any of your help," Leia said.

Lando gasped, "H-a-a-a . . ."

"What?" Leia said.

"It sounds like *Han*," said C-3PO, who had the best ear for languages.

Lando clutched at Chewbacca's wrists and rasped, "There's still a chance to save Han . . . at the East Platform."

Leia said, "Chewie," and the Wookiee released Lando. Still on his knees, Lando breathed hard, taking in deep lungfuls of air. As Leia and Chewbacca started running out of the corridor, he looked up to see C-3PO's parts bouncing in the net at Chewbacca's back.

"I'm terribly sorry about all this," C-3PO said as he moved away from Lando. "After all, he's only a Wookiee."

Even though he hadn't completely gotten his breath back, Lando rose from the floor and started running after the others. Leia was right: They had no reason to trust him. But if there was any chance of saving Han, Lando wanted to be there when it happened.

"Put Captain Solo in the cargo hold," Boba Fett instructed the two Cloud City guards. The guards guided the floating carbonite block up *Slave I*'s sloped landing ramp and through a narrow access hatch. Fett stood beside a stormtrooper on the landing ramp and kept his gaze on the walkway that extended from the landing platform. There was a door at the end of the walkway. If anyone came through the door before *Slave I* lifted off, Fett would see them.

Boba had already received payment from the Empire for tracking the *Millennium Falcon* to Cloud City, and he looked forward to collecting the bounty that Jabba the Hutt had placed on Solo. But Fett was well aware of the fact that other bounty hunters were still hoping to collect that bounty, and a lot could happen between Cloud City and Jabba's palace on Tatooine.

The guards exited the hatch and left with the stormtrooper. Boba Fett entered *Slave I*, locked the hatch behind him, and went to the cargo hold to secure his valuable merchandise.

With C-3PO's parts clattering in the net against his back, Chewbacca ran behind Leia as Lando led them around a curved terrace that overlooked the city. Leia and Chewbacca were armed with the blaster rifles that Lando had taken from the stormtroopers. The sky was red.

As they ran toward another corridor, C-3PO spotted a familiar droid in a nearby alcove. "Artoo!" the droid cried. "Artoo! Where have you been?"

Hearing C-3PO's words, Chewbacca stopped and turned around to bark at R2-D2, but his sudden action left C-3PO staring at the corridor wall.

C-3PO said, "Wait, turn around, you woolly —!" As Chewbacca turned to catch up with Leia and Lando, C-3PO was again able to see R2-D2, who was racing after the Wookiee. "Hurry, hurry!" C-3PO cried. "We're trying to save Han from the bounty hunter!"

R2-D2 whistled frantically after C-3PO.

"Well, at least you're still in one piece!" C-3PO replied, bouncing along at Chewbacca's back. "Look what happened to me!"

Leia was the first to reach the door to the East Platform. She ran through the doorway, followed by Chewbacca, but they stopped in their tracks as *Slave I* began to lift and rise away from the platform. Chewbacca roared and fired his blaster rifle, but the laser bolts glanced off the ship's energized shields.

Leia watched *Slave I* blast into the sky. The bounty hunter was getting away, doubtlessly heading for Tatooine. Leia had a horrible feeling that she might never see Han again.

"Oh, no!" C-3PO cried. "Chewie, they're behind you!"

Leia spun, and for once she was glad that C-3PO's

parts were dangling at Chewbacca's back. Otherwise, they might not have been aware until too late that they had been followed by the two stormtroopers.

The two were visible through the open doorway, in the corridor that had led to the East Platform. Lando jumped away from the doorway just as the stormtroopers fired, sending red blaster bolts over R2-D2's domed head and past Leia and Chewbacca. The Wookiee returned fire and felled a stormtrooper on his first shot, then squeezed off a series of bolts at the remaining stormtrooper while Lando and Leia darted back through the doorway, heading for a lift tube.

R2-D2 beeped nervously as the laser bolts sailed past his body. Chewbacca kept firing at the stormtrooper and moved fast after Leia and Lando. As the group hurried for a lift tube, Leia wondered again about Luke's fate.

Luke thought, *Doesn't Vader ever get tired?* He'd been engaged in battle with Darth Vader for several minutes, and the dark lord had not let up at all. Luke, on the other hand, was already sweating hard, and not just from the physical effort of the duel. All the steam was making the air in the chamber feel more humid than Dagobah's oppressive climate.

Yet Luke was holding up, matching Darth Vader's fighting prowess blow for blow. As steam billowed around them, Vader said, "You have learned much, young one."

"You'll find I'm full of surprises," Luke replied. He swung his lightsaber at Vader, and Vader swung back with enough power to knock Luke's weapon from his grip. Luke's lightsaber spun and fell away, then automatically deactivated as it clattered against the upper surface of the elevated platform.

Hoping to recover his lightsaber, Luke threw himself down the stairway, rolling painfully upon the metal steps until he landed on the metal platform. Darth Vader leaped into the air, passing over the steps to land with a loud *clang* near his opponent. Luke flinched at the sound, and looked up to see the tip of Vader's lightsaber dangling in front of his face.

Luke rose to his feet and backed away from Vader. *Where's my lightsaber? I can hardly see a thing down here!*

"Your destiny lies with me, Skywalker," Vader said as he slowly advanced toward Luke. "Obi-Wan knew this to be true."

"No!" Luke cried, then backed right into the open pit at the center of the raised platform.

"All too easy," Vader intoned.

At the bottom of the pit, Luke quickly struggled to his feet. He instantly recognized the metal columns inside the pit as freezing coils, and just as quickly knew he had to get out of the pit. Fast.

Still atop the elevated platform, Vader gestured at the nearby carbon-freezing controls and used the Force to pull a lever. Had Vader not looked away from the sudden blast of steam that erupted from the freezing pit, he might have seen Luke's form shoot from the pit to the ceiling.

Vader returned his gaze to the pit, waiting for the billowing steam to clear. Thinking Luke was frozen and that his words would go unheard, Vader said, "Perhaps you are not as strong as the Emperor thought."

There was a loud *clank* from overhead, and Vader looked up to see Luke clutching at a tangle of pipes and cables. "Impressive . . . most impressive," Vader commented, then raised his lightsaber and swung at a dangling hose. Steam blasted from the sliced ends of the hose, temporarily clouding Luke's vision.

But Luke flipped away from the ceiling and — on his way down — reached out with his left hand to grab a length of the sliced hose. Landing on his feet, he twisted the hose to spray steam directly into Vader's helmeted face. As the dark lord snarled and recoiled, Luke spotted his own lightsaber, resting on the other side of the platform. He extended the fingers of his right hand, and the lightsaber launched through the air and smacked into his palm. Vader swung his red-bladed lightsaber through the steam just as Luke ignited the blue beam of his own weapon. The lightsabers clashed as more steam flooded the chamber.

"Obi-Wan has taught you well," Vader said. "You have controlled your fear . . . now release your anger." He launched another attack, trying to goad Luke into unleashing his emotions. "Only your hatred can destroy me," he continued, swinging again at his opponent. But Luke leaped and executed a mid-air somersault, landing behind Vader. Vader was caught off guard as Luke lashed out with his lightsaber, and the dark lord backed up, stepping past the edge of the elevated platform.

Vader snarled as he fell to the darkness below.

With all the steam and noise on the platform, Luke was not surprised that he didn't hear Vader's impact. Luke peered over the edge and looked down, but saw no sign of Vader or his red lightsaber.

Luke thought, *Should I go after him?* Then he remembered Yoda's words: *Stopped they must be.*

Luke deactivated his lightsaber, clipped it to his belt, and jumped down into the darkness. Landing on the floor of the freezing chamber, he edged past a wall until he stood before a circular metal vent. The vent slid open, revealing a narrow, tubular tunnel that descended at a slight angle. *Another opening hatch and passage*, Luke observed. *Vader wants to lure me in.*

He entered the tunnel, walked through its short

length, and stepped down into a wide room. Behind him, a double hatch slid over the tunnel's opening. *He's trying to rattle my nerves. But I won't be rattled. If that tunnel's my only way out, my lightsaber will slice through the hatch.*

Luke moved across the room, searching for Darth Vader.

Vader stood in the shadows of the reactor control room and watched Luke walk toward a large circular window. Beyond the window was Cloud City's reactor shaft, a central wind tunnel nearly a kilometer in diameter.

Vader thought, *You were unwise to follow me down here. It would have been so much easier on you if you'd allowed yourself to be frozen in carbonite.*

Yes. Search the room for me. I'm not hiding. I'm right here. You see me now? Good.

Go on. Activate your lightsaber. The blue blade still looks so pure. Do you know I'm familiar with that particular weapon? The very one you're holding? The one that Obi-Wan must have given you. No, I don't believe you know that. Not yet.

Allow me to activate my own lightsaber. That's right . . . gaze at it, and believe that I'm preparing to strike. Don't mistake me . . . I am preparing to strike, but not with my lightsaber. I shall use the Force.

Pay no attention to the crack of metal behind you. That's just the sound of a pipe snapping from the wall and flying toward you. Ah! You dodged it. How clever.

But can you dodge this metal case? No, for it just struck the back of your head. Can you dodge this piece of machinery? No, it seems you could not. Can you dodge this . . . ?

A long, heavy piece of metal pipe traveled through the air, missing Luke's battered body but smashing through the large window. There was a sudden rush of air as the room depressurized, and a fierce wind tore at anything that wasn't bolted down, including Vader and Luke. As Vader's black cape tugged at his neck and shoulders, he reached out to grip the wall and watched as the wind lifted Luke off his feet and sucked him out through the shattered window, into Cloud City's reactor shaft.

Moments later, the wind died down, and Vader was able to release the wall. He stepped forward to the window, leaned over its jagged shards, and peered down to see Luke dangling from a gantry. He watched Luke pull himself up onto the gantry, and noticed that Luke had not lost his lightsaber during the fall.

Vader withdrew from the window. He thought, *The Emperor did not underestimate Luke Skywalker's strength. But I underestimated his will to live. I won't make that mistake again.*

As Vader made his way to a nearby lift tube, he decided it was time to relieve Luke of his lightsaber.

CHAPTER 18

Leia saw more stormtroopers coming up the corridor. She fired a burst of laser bolts at them, then darted up a short flight of steps to the waiting lift tube, which fortunately managed to hold her, Lando, Chewbacca, C-3PO's parts, and R2-D2.

The lift tube carried them to the corridor next to the *Millennium Falcon*'s landing platform. There was a control panel on the wall beside the door to the platform, and Lando ran to the panel and quickly punched in a coded sequence. Unfortunately, the code failed to open the door.

"The security code has been changed!" Lando exclaimed.

From Chewbacca's back, C-3PO said, "Artoo, you can tell the computer to override the security system."

R2-D2 beeped and scooted toward what appeared to be a computer terminal at the base of the control panel. The astromech popped open a panel and extended his computer interface arm as fast as he could, but not fast enough for the nervous C-3PO, who cried, "Artoo, hurry!"

Lando crossed the corridor to a comlink console, then entered his security code to address all parts of Cloud City. Holding the comlink, he said, "Attention! This is Lando Calrissian. The Empire has taken control of the city. I advise everyone to leave before more Imperial troops arrive."

As Lando turned from the comlink, there was a bright spark where R2-D2's arm met with the socket. R2-D2 screamed and smoke seeped out from under his domed head. Chewbacca grabbed hold of R2-D2 and tore him away from the wall.

"This way," Lando said, urging the group to follow him up the corridor.

R2-D2 beeped angrily and tried to move after the others, but accidentally smacked into the wall.

"Well, don't blame me," C-3PO said, bobbing along behind Chewbacca. "I'm an interpreter. I'm not supposed to know a power socket from a computer terminal."

R2-D2 regained control of himself but was still beeping with fury as he sped after his friends.

If Lando had wondered whether his broadcast message had reached the citizens of Cloud City, all doubts were dismissed as he ran into a crowded plaza, filled with people running for the public transport ships. Lando led Leia, Chewbacca, and R2-D2 to another door, and the astromech wasted no time in plugging his computer interface arm into a proper terminal socket.

Suddenly, they sighted approaching stormtroopers. As Leia and Chewbacca opened fire on the Imperial soldiers, R2-D2 rotated his dome and beeped at C-3PO, who — flailing against Chewbacca's back — was more immediately concerned about the blaster bolts that were whizzing past his head. "We're not interested in the hyperdrive on the *Millennium Falcon*," C-3PO shouted over the blaster fire. "It's fixed! Just open the door, you stupid lump."

More stormtroopers arrived, and Chewbacca, Leia, and Lando had to retreat down the corridor. They hadn't traveled far when R2-D2 let out a triumphant beep. The door slid open.

C-3PO shouted, "I never doubted you for a second. Wonderful!"

R2-D2 retracted his arm from the socket and waited until his friends had made it through the door. When he saw the stormtroopers advance from the corridor, he deployed his built-in fire extinguisher and sprayed opaque gas into the air. While the stormtroopers blundered through the smokescreen, R2-D2 moved through the door to the landing platform.

Despite R2-D2's efforts, a few stormtroopers managed to find their way to the open doorway. As Chewbacca neared the *Falcon*'s landing ramp, he tossed his pilfered blaster rifle to Lando. Lando took cover under the ship and fired at the stormtroopers, allowing Leia and R2-D2 time to make it to the ship.

The *Falcon*'s landing ramp was down. Unfortunately, Chewbacca forgot that C-3PO was strapped to his back. The droid's squirming didn't help either.

"Ouch!" C-3PO shouted as the back of his head struck the *Falcon*'s hull. "Oh! Ah! That hurt. Bend down, you thoughtless — ow!"

While Chewbacca and C-3PO bumped their way up the ramp, Leia turned to fire at the stormtroopers, who were now pouring out through the doorway. Lando saw R2-D2 scoot up the ramp and shouted, "Leia! Go!" Leia ran into the ship, with Lando at her heels.

Chewbacca had deposited the cargo net with C-3PO's parts on the floor before he ran into the cockpit and started flipping switches, energizing shields, and preparing for liftoff. As R2-D2 entered the *Falcon*, he extended a retractable claw to grab the cargo net and dragged C-3PO to a safer location.

C-3PO said, "I thought that hairy beast would be the end of me."

R2-D2 beeped.

"Of course, I've looked better," C-3PO grumbled.

Outside the *Falcon*, laser bolts glanced off the ship's shields as the stormtroopers continued to fire. But before the Imperials could do any serious damage, the *Falcon* lifted off the landing platform and roared away into the twilight sky.

Inside the Cloud City reactor shaft, Luke moved carefully along the gantry that was secured to a large, rudderlike vane. The vane was used to create desired changes in airflow, controlling the city's movements through Bespin's skies while routing Tibanna gas to processing facilities. Even though the gantry had a protective railing, Luke kept close to the vane and tried to shield his body from the strong, continuous wind that whipped through the deep shaft.

Luke edged around the vane to an open doorway that led into a narrow control room. The room was dark, only illuminated by the winking lights on the control consoles that lined the walls. Knowing that an activated lightsaber would reveal his position, Luke kept his weapon off as he stepped in.

Vader's close, he thought as he walked past the control consoles. *Dangerously close.*

Vader emerged sooner than Luke expected, leaping out from the shadows with his red lightsaber blazing. Luke jumped back and activated his own lightsaber's blue beam in time to block the attack.

217

But Vader swung wildly, slicing into machinery on either side of the narrow room as he drove Luke back through the open doorway.

Vader followed Luke onto the gantry, then brought his lightsaber down hard against Luke's blade. Luke stumbled and fell back against the metal-floored walkway that extended out to a cantilevered platform. He raised his gaze to find himself staring up the length of Vader's extended lightsaber.

"You are beaten," Vader said, looming above Luke. "It is useless to resist. Don't let yourself be destroyed as Obi-Wan did."

Remembering how Darth Vader had cut down Obi-Wan, Luke felt a sudden surge of strength, his face twisting with anger. He flicked his wrist and his lightsaber's blade whipped up, smacking Vader's blade aside and allowing Luke to quickly scramble to his feet. Vader lunged again with his weapon, and the two men exchanged a swift series of blows.

Luke swung hard and connected with the black armor plate on Vader's right shoulder. The Sith Lord snarled in pain as bright sparks exploded from the shoulder plate. But Vader never lost his grip on his lightsaber, and he swung again at Luke. Luke dodged the attack, darted past a vertical array of weather sensors at the platform's outer edge, then leaped to a beam that extended from the platform to another tall sensor array. Below the beam, the immense shaft fell away farther than his eyes could see.

Balancing on the beam, Luke turned as Vader's lightsaber sliced through the weather sensors. Luke raised his lightsaber to block another blow from Vader, but as his left hand clung to the damaged sensors and he struggled to maintain his footing, Vader's lightsaber lashed out again —

— and cut off Luke's right hand.

Luke screamed. His hand arced away from his right arm, carrying his lightsaber with it. The lightsaber automatically deactivated, and the weapon fell with the severed hand down into the shaft.

Vader moved forward to the edge of the platform and gazed down at Luke. Luke clutched his wounded arm to his chest and slumped down upon the beam.

"There is no escape," Vader said as Luke moved away from him, crawling backward to the outermost sensor array. "Don't make me destroy you."

But Luke kept crawling. He felt dizzy and sick. His only goal was to put distance between himself and Vader.

Seeing that Luke was utterly defeated, Vader switched off his lightsaber. "You do not yet realize your importance," Vader continued. "You have only begun to discover your power. Join me and I will complete your training. With our combined strength, we can end this destructive conflict and bring order to the galaxy."

Reaching the end of the beam, Luke wrapped his arms around the outermost sensor array. Turning to face Vader, he screamed, "I'll never join you!"

"If only you knew the power of the dark side," Vader said, reaching out to clutch the air with his black-gloved fist. "Obi-Wan never told you what happened to your father."

"He told me enough!" Luke said as he wrapped his arms around the sensor array and lowered his feet to a metal ring. Wincing, he added, "He told me you killed him."

"No," Vader said, his fist still clenched. "I *am* your father."

Luke's eyes went wide. *My father? But Ben told me . . .*

"No," Luke whimpered. "No. That's not true! That's impossible!"

"Search your feelings," Vader said. "You know it to be true."

"No!" Luke shouted. "No!"

The wind picked up, and Vader's black cape rippled at his back. "Luke. You can destroy the Emperor. He has foreseen this. It is your destiny." He opened his left hand and held it out to Luke. "Join me, and together we can rule the galaxy as father and son."

His voice is so hypnotic, Luke thought, and felt part of himself falling under Vader's spell. But only part of him. Luke looked down into the deep shaft that seemed to stretch down to forever.

"Come with me," Vader urged. "It is the only way."

Luke looked directly at Vader and felt a certain calmness as he thought, *No. It's not the only way.*

Then Vader watched in astonishment as Luke released his arms from the sensor array and fell, down, down into the reactor shaft.

There was nothing to break Luke's fall. As he tumbled through the air, he looked up, half expecting to see Darth Vader leap down after him. But all he saw of Vader was a rapidly receding black speck at the edge of the already distant vane.

Suddenly, Luke was aware that he was no longer falling straight down. Twisting his body, he saw that he was caught in a powerful air current that was drawing him toward an open exhaust pipe in the shaft's wall.

Luke sailed into the exhaust pipe, a metal-lined tubular tunnel that twisted down and away from the reactor shaft. The pipe's walls were smooth, sending Luke on an uncontrolled slide until he entered what seemed to be a dip in the pipe, and slowed to a stop. But before he could plan his next move, a trap-door dropped open beneath him, plunging him down another pipe.

Luke's mind raced, trying to figure out where the second pipe would carry him. As the pipe twisted into an almost vertical slope, he guessed the pipes were designed to expel stray matter from the reactor shaft. He extended his limbs in an attempt to slow his descent, but the effort was too much for his drained, battered body. He continued to slide.

The pipe terminated at a retractable hatch, and as Luke's body neared it, the hatch opened. Luke fell through the open hole and slammed into some spindly horizontal metal bars. He desperately grabbed at the bars and caught them.

He realized he was clutching at an electronic weather vane that was secured to the wide under-side of Cloud City. Below Luke, there was nothing but clouds.

Luke felt so helpless. Then he thought of the spirit of Obi-Wan, who had come to his aid before, and he gasped, "Ben . . . Ben, please!"

But Ben had said he could not interfere if Luke chose to face Vader, and so there would be no response.

Luke's muscles strained as he struggled to get a better hold on the weather vane. He looked up to the hatch from which he'd been ejected. The hatch was still open. He began to shimmy up the weather vane, but as he reached for the hatch door, the door automatically lifted and locked in place.

Then Luke slipped down the weather vane, but somehow caught the horizontal bars with his legs so that he dangled upside down. The pain was almost unbearable.

"Ben," Luke cried again. But when Ben did not answer, Luke thought of the one other person who might be able to help him. "Leia!" he cried out.

He didn't even know if Leia was still on Cloud City, or if she was in any position to help him. Still, he clung to the weather vane, searched the surrounding clouds, and yelled, "Hear me! Leia!"

The *Millennium Falcon* was flying fast away from Cloud City but had not yet left Bespin's upper atmosphere when Leia heard Luke's voice. She was sitting in the pilot's seat, looking through the cockpit window, and at first she thought the voice was just some trick of her imagination. But then an image formed in her mind, an image of Luke, injured and dangling from some kind of metal array at the bottom of Cloud City.

"Luke . . ." Leia said. Then she turned to her right, where Chewbacca sat behind his controls. She said, "We've got to go back."

Lando was standing in the area behind Chewbacca's and Leia's seats. Lando had just informed Leia that the *Falcon*'s sensors had detected the approach of TIE fighters, so he was surprised by Leia's sudden decision. He said, "What?"

"I know where Luke is," Leia said.

"But what about those fighters?" Lando asked.

Leia commanded, "Chewie, just do it."

As Chewbacca reset his controls, Lando said, "But what about Vader?"

Chewbacca roared at Lando.

"All right, all right, all right," Lando said, knowing better than to argue with the Wookiee.

The *Falcon* looped around a wide cloud formation and sped back to Cloud City.

Darth Vader strode through a white-walled corridor in Cloud City. An Imperial officer and a squad of stormtroopers traveled in his wake as he headed for his shuttle's landing platform. "Alert the Star Destroyer to prepare for my arrival," he said to the officer, then walked toward his tall *Lambda*-class shuttle.

Vader knew Luke had not perished in the reactor shaft. *If he had, I would have sensed it.* Vader would have searched for Luke himself, but upon learning that Princess Leia and Lando Calrissian had escaped in the *Millennium Falcon*, and that Imperial scanners had detected the *Falcon* was now returning to Cloud City, Vader had revised his plan. He would return to the *Executor*, and allow the princess to rescue Luke.

Then Darth Vader would capture them all.

The *Falcon* soared closer to Cloud City, and Lando was the first to sight the figure that dangled like a broken doll from the electronic weather vane. "Look, someone's up there," he said, pointing a finger to direct Chewbacca's and Leia's gaze.

"It's Luke," Leia said. He looked like he was about to fall. Leia tried to remain calm as she said, "Chewie, slow down. Slow down and we'll get under him. Lando, open the top hatch."

As Lando ran out of the cockpit and went to the hydraulic lift, Chewbacca jockeyed the ship under Luke. Luke caught a brief glimpse of Leia in the cockpit, then saw the top hatch slide open to reveal Lando.

"Okay," Leia said as the Wookiee closed the distance between the *Falcon*'s hull and Cloud City's bottom. Chewbacca barked, and Leia said, "Easy, Chewie."

Luke didn't know Lando, but because he'd arrived with Leia, Luke trusted he was an ally. The moment the *Falcon*'s hatch was positioned beneath him, Luke let go of the weather vane and fell into his arms.

"Lando?" Leia said into the ship's comm.

Lando answered, "Okay, let's go."

Leia watched Chewbacca paw the controls and the *Falcon* dropped away from the bottom of Cloud City. Just then, the Wookiee saw three Imperial TIE fighters approaching at high speed.

Leia climbed out of her seat and found Lando supporting Luke in the passage tube behind the cockpit. Lando had wrapped a blanket around Luke, and Leia felt crushed as she imagined the beating Luke had obviously endured. She took Luke in her arms, allowing Lando to enter the cockpit and scramble into the pilot's seat.

Luke moaned, "Oh, Leia."

Suddenly, Imperial-fired flak exploded outside the ship.

"All right, Chewie," Lando said. "Let's go."

The Wookiee aimed for some distant clouds, increased power to the thrusters, and launched the ship away from the oncoming TIE fighters.

As the *Falcon* hurtled forward, Leia moved Luke to a bunk and broke out the ship's emergency medical supplies. She worked fast and did her best to treat his wounds, and didn't ask for details when she placed the autotourniquet on his right arm. But Leia suspected she'd be needed in the cockpit, so when Luke was stabilized, she kissed him and said, "I'll be back."

Leia entered the cockpit and took the navigator's seat behind Lando. Both Chewbacca and Lando were flipping switches and adjusting controls as they tried to shake off the TIE fighters that were now hammering the *Falcon*'s deflector shields with their lasers. As the *Falcon* entered space, Leia saw a large, wedge-shaped ship in orbit of Bespin, and said, "Star Destroyer."

It was Vader's ship, the *Executor*.

"All right, Chewie," Lando said. "Ready for lightspeed."

"*If* your people fixed the hyperdrive," Leia pointed out. After all, she'd been disappointed by the *Falcon*'s hyperdrive twice before.

Ignoring Leia's remark, Lando said, "All the coordinates are set. It's now or never."

Chewbacca barked.

Lando ordered, "Punch it!"

The Wookiee pulled back on the throttle. The engine sounded like it was winding up, then it cut off.

"They told me they fixed it," Lando said as Chewbacca let out a frustrated howl. "I trusted them to fix it."

More flak exploded outside the *Falcon*. Leia sat

back in her seat and glared at Lando. Chewbacca jumped out of his seat and stormed out of the cockpit.

"It's not my fault!" Lando insisted.

After returning to the *Executor*, Darth Vader proceeded to the bridge and walked directly to Admiral Piett's command station. Snapping to attention at the sight of Vader, Piett announced, "They'll be in range of our tractor beam in moments, lord."

Vader asked, "Did your men deactivate the hyperdrive on the *Millennium Falcon*?"

"Yes, my lord," Piett reported. He knew if his men hadn't done their job, he'd be a dead man.

"Good," Vader said. "Prepare a boarding party and set your weapons for stun."

"Yes, my lord."

Seated on a crate in the *Millennium Falcon*'s main hold, C-3PO was almost entirely reassembled except for his lower left leg, which he held across his lap. Since boarding the *Falcon*, R2-D2 had been working as fast as he could to put his friend back together, and was now using a retractable tool to repair C-3PO's right foot.

Chewbacca ran into the hold and grunted loudly to himself. C-3PO remarked, "Noisy brute. Why don't we just go into lightspeed?"

While Chewbacca lifted the deck plates to uncover the access pit, R2-D2 beeped his explanation.

"We can't?" C-3PO said. "How would you know the hyperdrive is deactivated?"

As Chewbacca jumped into the pit, R2-D2 whistled knowingly.

"The city's central computer told you?" said C-3PO, surprised. "Artoo-Detoo, you know better than to trust a strange computer."

R2-D2's extended repair tool sparked against the golden droid's right foot.

"Ouch!" C-3PO cried. "Pay attention to what you're doing!"

In the pit, Chewbacca confronted the hyperdrive with a fusioncutter. There was an unexpected flash of electric current, triggering a surge that caused sparks to fly in the *Falcon*'s cockpit.

On the bridge of the *Executor*, Vader gazed through the viewport and watched the *Falcon* attempt to evade the pursuing TIE fighters. Focusing his attention on the ship that carried the young Skywalker, he said aloud, "Luke."

On the *Falcon*, Luke's head lifted from his bunk. He said, "Father."

Son, Vader said from across space, *come with me.*

Luke's head fell back to the bunk. "Ben," he moaned, "why didn't you tell me?" Then the ship's hull shuddered. Luke rose from his bunk, taking the blanket with him, and proceeded to the cockpit.

In the cockpit, Lando shouted into the comm, "Chewie!"

In the main hold's access pit, Chewbacca heard Lando and angrily smashed the fusioncutter against the hyperdrive mechanism.

Back in the cockpit, Lando and Leia looked up in surprise as Luke entered. Wrapped in the blanket, he gazed out the cockpit at the *Executor* and said, "It's Vader."

Then Luke heard Vader's voice again from across space: *Luke . . . it is your destiny.*

Luke sank back into the seat behind Leia. He closed his eyes and groaned again, "Ben, why didn't you tell me?"

The *Executor* was closing in on the *Millennium Falcon*. Admiral Piett turned to a lieutenant and said, "Alert all commands. Ready for the tractor beam."

"Artoo, come back at once!" C-3PO cried in the *Falcon*'s main hold. "You haven't finished with me yet!" Indeed, C-3PO was still holding his left leg. As R2-

D2 scooted past the access pit that contained the furious Chewbacca and over to the main engineering console, C-3PO said, "You don't know how to fix the hyperdrive. Chewbacca can do it. I'm standing here in pieces, and you're having delusions of grandeur!"

R2-D2 extended his manipulator arm to move a circuit on a control panel. Suddenly, the control panel lit up, and the hyperdrive kicked in.

"You did it!" C-3PO shouted as the entire ship tilted up, sending R2-D2 rolling backward into the open pit to fall on top of Chewbacca. The hyperdrive engines roared.

In the cockpit, Luke was already seated, but Leia and Lando were nearly thrown off their feet as the ship blasted into hyperspace.

In the blink of an eye, the *Millennium Falcon* was gone. On the *Executor's* bridge, Admiral Piett gasped, then looked at Darth Vader and cringed.

Vader was still facing the viewport, gazing at the area where the *Millennium Falcon* had been just moments before escaping into hyperspace. He turned slowly, then proceeded across the walkway, away from the viewport. Below Vader, the technicians in the bridge's lower level looked up at him, waiting for him to react to the situation.

Maintaining his slow stride, Vader glanced to his

right and barely noticed Admiral Piett. The Sith Lord could practically taste the Imperial officer's fear, but as angry as he was at losing Luke, he knew that Piett — unlike some recently deceased Imperial officers — was not at fault. Vader had much to contemplate, so he looked away from Piett and kept walking.

Without a word, he left the bridge.

CHAPTER 20

The Rebel fleet was traveling through space, en route to what the Rebel Alliance hoped would be their new secret base. X-wing and Y-wing starfighters cruised past some of the larger vessels, including a three-hundred-meter-long Nebulon-B escort frigate, which had been converted for medical duty.

A single ship was attached to the Nebulon-B's docking tube: the *Millennium Falcon*. In the *Falcon*'s cockpit, Lando Calrissian was in the pilot's seat. As Chewbacca entered the cockpit, Lando spoke into his comlink, "Luke, we're ready for takeoff."

Luke's voice answered, "Good luck, Lando."

Lando said, "When we find Jabba the Hutt and that bounty hunter, we'll contact you."

Luke answered into his own comlink, "I'll meet you at the rendezvous point on Tatooine." Showered and wearing a clean white robe, Luke was sitting on an elevated bed in the Nebulon-B's surgery suite. The bed was adjusted to an upright position so he could watch 2-1B, the medical droid, who stood to his right. At the foot of his bed, Leia stood quietly, listening to Luke's conversation with Lando.

From Luke's comlink, Lando's voice said, "Princess, we'll find Han. I promise."

Luke thought Leia might say something, but she remained silent, so he said into his comlink, "Chewie, I'll be waiting for your signal."

The Wookiee wailed over the comlink.

Luke said, "Take care, you two. May the Force be with you."

Chewbacca's wail was heard again over the comlink, which brought a smile to Leia's face. Luke grinned back at her, but then Leia's smile seemed to melt away into an expression of sadness.

No, not sadness, Luke thought as she stepped away from him. *She's devastated. Devastated about Han.*

Leia moved across the room to join R2-D2 and the fully repaired C-3PO, who were facing a wide viewport. Luke turned his attention back to 2-1B's surgical work. At Luke's right wrist, there was an open panel that exposed the working mechanisms for his new hand, a realistic-looking synthetic replica that the droid had already attached to the end of Luke's arm.

Testing the hand's artificial nerve connections, 2-1B prodded the fingers with a thin metal pin. "Ow!" Luke said, feeling the pin's contact. Luke wriggled the fingers, made a fist, then relaxed his hand. It was completely functional.

Luke rose from the bed and stepped over beside Leia and the droids. He followed their gaze out the viewport and watched the deployed *Millennium Falcon* glide past and away from the medical frigate. He put his arm around Leia's back and held her to his side, hoping to comfort her, then he realized he was touching her shoulder with his new hand.

R2-D2 whistled as the *Falcon* flew out of sight. Still standing by Leia, Luke thought about the future. *Will we be able to rescue Han? Why didn't Ben tell me the truth? And what will I do if . . . no, not if. What will I do when I next meet Darth Vader?*

My father.

The future had once seemed so promising to Luke, but now everything seemed uncertain and complicated. What had Yoda said? *Always in motion is the future.*

The medical frigate and the rest of the Rebel fleet slowly veered onto a different course, then continued on into space.

Like his father, Anakin Skywalker, Luke Skywalker had a future to think about.